The Plot to Kill a Queen

A ROYAL SPY STORY IN THREE ACTS

ALSO BY DEBORAH HOPKINSON

Race Against Death: The Greatest POW Rescue of World War II

The Deadliest Fires Then and Now

The Deadliest Hurricanes Then and Now

The Deadliest Diseases Then and Now

We Must Not Forget: Holocaust Stories of Survival and Resistance

We Had to Be Brave: Escaping the Nazis on the Kindertransport

D-Day: The World War II Invasion That Changed History

Dive! World War II Stories of Sailors & Submarines in the Pacific

Courage & Defiance: Stories of Spies, Saboteurs, and Survivors in World War II Denmark

Titanic: Voices from the Disaster

Up Before Daybreak: Cotton and People in America

Shutting Out the Sky: Life in the Tenements of New York, 1880–1924

The Plot to Kill a Queen

A Royal Spy Story in Three Acts

❧ Also including ❧

The Princess Saves the Cakes
A One-Act Play to Perform with a Company of Friends

DEBORAH HOPKINSON

Scholastic Press
New York

Copyright © 2023 by Deborah Hopkinson

All rights reserved. Published by Scholastic Press, an imprint of Scholastic Inc., *Publishers since 1920*. SCHOLASTIC, SCHOLASTIC PRESS, and associated logos are trademarks and/or registered trademarks of Scholastic Inc.

The publisher does not have any control over and does not assume any responsibility for author or third-party websites or their content.

No part of this publication may be reproduced, stored in a retrieval system, or transmitted in any form or by any means, electronic, mechanical, photocopying, recording, or otherwise, without written permission of the publisher. For information regarding permission, write to Scholastic Inc., Attention: Permissions Department, 557 Broadway, New York, NY 10012.

While inspired by real events and historical characters, this is a work of fiction and does not claim to be historically accurate or portray factual events or relationships. Please keep in mind that references to actual persons, living or dead, business establishments, events, or locales may not be factually accurate, but rather fictionalized by the author.

Library of Congress Cataloging-in-Publication Data

Names: Hopkinson, Deborah, author.
Title: The plot to kill a queen : a royal spy story in three acts, also including the Princess saves the cakes, a one-act play to perform with a company of friends / Deborah Hopkinson.
Description: First edition. | New York : Scholastic Press, 2023. | Audience: Ages 8–12. | Audience: Grades 4–6. | Summary: In 1582 thirteen-year-old Emilia Bassano is a lute player and aspiring playwright who stumbles on a plot to kill Queen Elizabeth, and is recruited by Sir Francis Walsingham to go to the castle where Mary Queen of Scots is being held and discover who is responsible for the plot.
Identifiers: LCCN 2023000509 | ISBN 9781338660586 (hardcover) | ISBN 9781338660593 (ebook)
Subjects: LCSH: Elizabeth I, Queen of England, 1533-1603—Juvenile fiction. | Mary, Queen of Scots, 1542-1587—Juvenile fiction. | Walsingham, Francis, Sir, 1532-1590—Juvenile fiction. | Lutenists—Juvenile fiction. | Assassination—Juvenile fiction. | Conspiracies—Great Britain—History—16th century—Juvenile fiction. | Spy stories. | Great Britain—History—Elizabeth, 1558-1603—Juvenile fiction. | CYAC: Elizabeth I, Queen of England, 1533-1603—Fiction. | Mary, Queen of Scots, 1542-1587—Fiction. | Walsingham, Francis, Sir, 1532-1590—Fiction. | Lutenists—Fiction. | Assassination—Fiction. | Conspiracies—Fiction. | Spies—Fiction. | Great Britain—History—Elizabeth, 1558-1603—Fiction. | BISAC: JUVENILE FICTION / Historical / Europe | JUVENILE FICTION / People & Places / Europe | LCGFT: Historical fiction. | Spy fiction.
Classification: LCC PZ7.H788125 Plo 2023 | DDC 813.54 [Fic]—dc23/eng/20230110
LC record available at https://lccn.loc.gov/2023000509

10 9 8 7 6 5 4 3 2 1   23 24 25 26 27

Printed in Italy   183
First edition, October 2023

Book design by Abby Dening

Illustration, page i—Elizabeth I (1533-1603).
Illustration, page iii—Elizabeth I coronation portrait; unknown artist, around 1600; probably a copy of lost original from 1559.

Sheffield Castle was the gloomiest, smelliest, dreariest medieval castle you ever saw. If Mary, Queen of Scots, couldn't escape, how could I?

AS FOR MY OWN PART I CARE NOT FOR DEATH...
―Elizabeth I

Queen Elizabeth once declared she cared nothing for death. I've never felt that way. Especially that morning, when death was chasing at my heels.

It was cold. I ran, frosty fog stinging my cheeks. But I was glad for this thick, swirling curtain. It had helped me get nearly all the way across the bridge without being seen. Now, though, I heard shouts and the *clomp, clomp, clomping* of heavy boots behind me.

All my choices were bad. If I jumped, I'd plunge into the dark, stinking waters of the moat. (*Pee-ew!* The castle toilets emptied into it.)

I could try running through the deer park and across the open fields to Sheffield. If I reached the Rose and Crown Inn, I could get a coach back to London. But could

I make it that far? Once the autumn mist burned off, I'd be spotted. There weren't enough old oaks to hide me.

You'll be quite safe, the spymaster had promised.

I'd never felt safe here.

Then just as I was about to turn and give myself up, I saw a chance. A slim one, but a chance.

"Hold on, Mouse," I whispered, tightening the wrap that kept the little spaniel safe and snug against my chest.

And then . . .

Oh, wait! I seem to have started my story in the wrong place. This scene belongs in Act II; no, probably Act III. Not here at the beginning. So let's try another way.

Imagine you're entering a playhouse. Found a good spot? Excellent. Settle in, then turn the page. Glance at the playbill to see who's who and what's ahead.

But don't tarry too long: The curtain is about to rise.

> A **playbill**, or program, is given out or sold at events such as theater performances. It provides the audience with information about the production and players.

The Plot to Kill a Queen

A ROYAL SPY STORY IN THREE ACTS

—— Also featuring ——

The Princess Saves the Cakes
A One-Act Play to Perform with a Company of Friends

ACT I
Uneasy Lies the Head That Wears a Crown

ACT II
The Play's the Thing

ACT III
Vigilant as a Cat

THERE WILL BE TWO INTERMISSIONS, OR INTERVALS, BETWEEN THE ACTS.

The Princess Saves the Cakes
follows the production notes

Cast
IN ORDER OF APPEARANCE*

Emilia Bassano (me!), thirteen, lute player, aspiring playwright

Mouse *(also Mousekin or Mousie)*, three, sweet dog with long ears and small brain

Horace, thirteen, cook's apprentice, Whitehall Palace

William Shakespeare, eighteen, theater lover visiting London from the countryside

Frances Walsingham, fifteen, daughter of Sir Francis, friend of Emilia

Elizabeth, forty-nine, Queen of England and Ireland

Thomas Phillips, twenty-six, linguist and code expert, assistant to Sir Francis Walsingham

Sir Francis Walsingham, fifty, secretary of state and Elizabeth's spymaster

Ursula, Lady Walsingham, fifty, described by Sir Frances as his most kind and loving wife

Mrs. E. Hughes, age unknown, chaperone

Daniel, Sheffield innkeeper

Andrew Melville of Garvock, forty-nine, master of the household of Mary, Queen of Scots

Bessie Pierrepont, fourteen, favored English attendant of Mary, Queen of Scots

Rebecca Alice (Alice), twelve, English maidservant at Sheffield Castle

Mary, Queen of Scots, forty, deposed queen of Scotland, cousin of Queen Elizabeth

Geddon, age unknown, a royal terrier

Elizabeth Curle, age unknown, trusted Scottish lady-in-waiting to Mary, Queen of Scots

Claude Nau, age unknown, French confidential secretary to Mary, Queen of Scots

Bess of Hardwick, age fifty-five, Mary's keeper, along with her husband, the Earl of Shrewsbury

Nathan, fifteen, innkeeper's son

---

* *Names in bold were inspired by historical figures of the sixteenth century, except in the case of Mouse, who is modeled on Little Rue, a twenty-first-century spaniel. Other cast members are fictitious.*

A note on forms of address: In Elizabethan England most women, whether married or unmarried, were addressed as Mistress, *abbreviated as* Mrs. *The term* Miss *for unmarried women was not yet in use (nor was* Ms., *now used for both). Here we will use* Mrs. *for married women and* Mistress *for unmarried girls and women.*

Notes from the producers and a timeline follow the main production. The play The Princess Saves the Cakes *may be freely copied without permissions for use in a classroom, backyard, or perhaps even an inn courtyard. Break a leg!*

Prologue
(DON'T SKIP IT)

> A prologue is a speech or introduction at the beginning of a play or book.

"What's past is prologue."
—William Shakespeare, *The Tempest*,
Act II, Scene 1

Now we start again, properly this time, with a prologue. Prologues are quite useful. At least they were in 1582, when the tale I am about to tell took place. Back then, crowds flocked to the courtyards of inns to watch plays. People chatted and munched on nuts, pippin apples, and oysters. A prologue helped get their attention and quiet the crowd so the play could begin.

Of course, as a respectable thirteen-year-old female, I wasn't supposed to go to playhouses alone. More women attended plays after the Globe Theatre opened in 1599. Yet even as I write these words years later (in 1623), only men and boys with white skin are allowed to perform onstage. That's all very well for them, I suppose, but what about the rest of us? I wonder if things will be different (and better) in your time, whenever that may be.

As you'll soon find, I've always been prone to "wonderings." I especially wonder about other times, past and future. That's one reason I'll leave this tale with my papers, hoping it may be found someday. Otherwise, I expect my name will be lost to history—unlike Will Shakespeare, whom you're about to meet.

I imagine you know Shakespeare's name. If you do, it's partly thanks to Will's friends, who've just published a collection of thirty-six of his plays: the First Folio. I bought a bound copy, though it was dear at one pound. His work is quite marvelous, really. And if any First Folios survive into the future, I suspect they'll cost more than a pound.

Of course, we can't all be Shakespeare. That doesn't mean our stories don't count. In fact, I believe our stories matter more, because honestly, if we don't tell them, who will?

So, I beg you, please tell your story. Write it down for people in the future to read. Why not? That's a question I ask a lot. I hope you'll ask it too, especially when you're told you're not allowed to do something.

Well, that's enough for the prologue. One last thing: Feel free to munch on nuts to your heart's content.

Just remember to pick up the shells—especially if you're reading in bed.

—*Emilia Bassano Lanyer*
London, 1623

❦ Act I ❦
Uneasy Lies the Head That Wears a Crown

"UNEASY LIES THE HEAD THAT WEARS A CROWN."
–William Shakespeare, Henry IV, Part 2, Act III, Scene 1

> An **act** is a division or section in a play.
> To **act** means to perform.

One

Act I, Scene 1, A deserted storeroom in Whitehall Palace, late September, 1582

"This is a bad choice, Emilia," said Horace. "A very bad choice. I wanted to come, but now I can't get away. Why plunge ahead without me? Can't you wait till I have a free afternoon?"

"And when will that be?" I demanded, reaching out to brush a speck of flour off his cheek. "You work under cooks with tempers like blazing fires. They treat you horribly, despite your talents. Why, Queen Elizabeth herself loves your gingerbread.

"Besides, winter will be here soon and I might not get another chance, so it has to be today," I went on (though that wasn't the whole truth). "Horace, I know you can understand how much this means to me better than almost anyone," I continued. "Why, look at how devoted you are to learning to cook! And I won't be alone, will I, Mouse?"

Woof! My frisky long-eared spaniel barked and twirled in a circle. She could always sense when an outside adventure—or a treat—was at hand.

"But I'd better hurry or I'll be late," I told Horace. "Because *you're* late."

"It's been so busy since Her Majesty added more guests for tonight's dinner," Horace explained. "Also . . ."

"Also, admit it: You got lost," I teased. I'd asked Horace to meet me in an old storeroom tucked away in a deserted wing of Whitehall Palace's vast labyrinth of buildings. It was near a little-used rear entrance: I didn't want to be spotted coming or going.

"It's easy for you, Em," Horace protested. "You practically grew up at Whitehall, trailing after your father whenever he played at court."

"That's true." I smiled a little, thinking of Papa. It had been six years since he passed away, but I thought of him every day. I missed his warm brown eyes, which twinkled when he laughed. I missed the sound of his rich voice, singing me gently to sleep. I missed the way he guided my fingers so patiently when he taught me to play the lute.

And, especially lately, I'd been thinking of those

magical evenings during holiday festivities, when Queen Elizabeth invited the children of courtiers, musicians, and servants to hear music and watch theatricals. I would look up at the musicians' gallery and Papa would smile down at me. How proud I felt!

"Most fathers would've left a motherless little one with a nursemaid, but Papa always brought me along," I told Horace now. "He said I was his bright candle, and he needed me to light his way."

Horace pointed. "That was his lute, wasn't it?"

"Yes, he brought it from Italy and taught me to play on it. He made the wooden carrying case and strap himself. There's even a special pocket inside to hold pages of music," I said, stashing my instrument carefully behind some crates for later. "Now, if you hold Mousekin, I'll take that packet. Did you find everything, even boots?"

"The boots are the best part, Em, fine leather and not too worn," Horace said, batting away Mouse's wet tongue as she tried to lick more flour off his face. My little dog would eat anything.

"I still think it's a bad idea," Horace said again. "You get these notions in your head, Em, and you forge ahead without thinking things through. Remember that time we got caught sneaking into the tiltyard to try on armor and . . ."

"It will be *fine*," I cut him off. "And don't worry; if I'm found out, I won't let on who got me the disguise. I don't want you to lose your place."

Horace had worked in the palace kitchens ever since I'd known him. He'd never shared anything about his family or past. I only knew that, like me, he was thirteen. And I knew he dreamed of being a master cook someday.

As for my dreams, well, this day was part of making them happen. And I had made up my mind to go, whether Horace joined me or not.

"Will you be back in time to perform?" Horace asked.

"Aye, the Bell Savage Inn is just on Ludgate Hill. I'll come back here to change, then join my cousin Arthur and his musicians in plenty of time," I said, tearing open the parcel. "Oh, marvelous!"

Horace had found a boy's cap, a short walking cloak, hose, a pair of breeches, and just as he'd said, a very fine pair of boots made for work or walking—boots far sturdier than my fancy velvet pumps with soft leather soles.

"Emilia, what if Sir Francis finds out?"

"Horace, stop fretting. No one will find out!" I snapped, slipping behind some stacked barrels to change. "I'm not even sure I'll tell Fannie."

"You won't tell Fannie? I thought Frances Walsingham was like a sister to you," Horace protested.

"She is. But . . . but there's no sense taking the chance she'll tell her parents," I said. "I know they wouldn't approve. And I don't want to anger my benefactors: I owe Sir Francis and Lady Walsingham a lot for taking me in after Papa died and letting me study with Fannie's tutor.

"I love my Bassano cousins, but if I had to live with Cousin Arthur and his wife, I'd never read another book again, Horace. They already have three children under five. Why, I'd spend my days wiping babies' bottoms!"

"You can't be sure Sir Francis won't find out, Emilia," Horace argued. "They say he knows *everything* that goes on in England and has a network of intelligence gatherers as vast as stars in the sky."

"I can well believe it. His office is in the house and we see all sorts of people coming and going from Seething Lane, day and night," I said as I wriggled into my disguise. "Fannie worries her father is working himself to death trying to protect the queen from plots against her life."

I folded my own clothes and placed them in the bottom of my leather satchel. It felt strange not to have petticoats and a long gown floating around me. Strange, but wonderful. *I can even run if I want to—or have to*, I thought.

"I love these boots! Now, are you ready to see me transformed?" I jumped out.

WOOO! WOOO! Mousekin howled in alarm, lifting her small black muzzle to the sky.

"Even Mouse doesn't know you," Horace laughed. "You look every bit a servant lad. Be careful, though, to keep your long curls tucked under the cap."

I opened the door and we looked both ways. The corridor was empty. Moments later, we stepped outside.

"I've got to get back," said Horace. "Promise you'll be careful, Em."

"I'll blend into the crowd like a mouse at a great feast. And if anyone does bother me, I have *this* Mouse to protect me."

"That I'd like to see. Off you go, Mousie." Horace handed over my favorite bundle of fur. "Be a good girl for your mistress—and don't you get into trouble either."

Act I, Scene 2, On muddy London roads

Once we were on the road heading toward Ludgate Hill, I arranged my walking cloak so only Mouse's muzzle and eyes stuck out.

"I only have a penny left, and that's for our entrance fee, Mousie," I whispered. "So we'll have to walk—no river ferry today. And we definitely don't have time for you to stop and sniff."

London's roads were so bad, most people got around the city on boats that carried people up and down the River

The Plot to Kill a Queen

Thames. But I'd given Horace nearly all my savings to buy a disguise.

"Now, Mousekin, I'm sorry to tell you, but this also means we have no money for treats. You'll have to do without a hot pie." Despite her small size, Mouse had the appetite of a wolfhound.

It had rained hard in the night and the road was little more than a stream of churned-up mire. Wagon and cart drivers struggled to keep their loads from overturning. I was stepping around a puddle when a man yelled, "Watch out!"

The best way to travel from Whitehall Palace to Ludgate Hill was by boat on the Thames, but I'd spent all my coins on a disguise.

Deborah Hopkinson

My little Mouse: sweet, loyal, and brave (though not very bright).

Whirling, I saw a large bay horse lurching toward me, its hooves slipping in slick mud. It pulled a wagon piled high with cabbages from the countryside. The heavy cart listed to one side like a boat on choppy waters.

"It's about to tip!" someone shouted.

I jumped out of the way, smashing into a large woman balancing a basket of laundry on her hip. Startled, she shoved me with her other hand. I fell, slipping to one knee in the puddle.

Woof! Woof! Mouse howled in fright and squirmed like a wriggling eel. "No!" I yelled, holding her tight. "You'll be trampled!"

The Plot to Kill a Queen

Thankfully, the wagon righted itself just as a skinny boy leaned close to help me up—close enough to pick the small cloth purse that hung from a leather cord from my belt.

∞

So what set all the events of this tale in motion?

Was it the horse; the cart; my scared, squirming spaniel?

Or perhaps it was me, with all my rushing and scheming—doing whatever it took to get to the Bell Savage Inn that day.

You see, I'd fallen under the spell of the stage. And I couldn't let anything stop me from seeing a play.

Two

🖋 **Act I, Scene 3, Courtyard of the Bell Savage Inn, Ludgate Hill**

"Penny to see the play." A gatherer at the entrance thrust his money pot under my nose. "No entry without a penny. Make haste, now. Slide it into the slot."

I shifted Mouse into the crook of my left arm and fumbled for the coin in my bag. That's when I discovered it was gone. *Alack!* I knew thieves roamed the city like invisible ghosts with hungry fingers. I should've guessed that boy hadn't stopped simply to be kind.

"Oh, please, sir," I begged. "Someone has snatched my penny. Can't you let me in, just this once? I don't take up much space."

Mouse, bless her heart, joined in, whining pitifully. No use.

"Move along!" grumbled the man behind me in line.

The Plot to Kill a Queen

"The church bells will soon strike two. I want to find a good place to stand."

I stepped out of the queue. I felt hot tears sting my cheeks. I'd worked so hard to get here. Now what?

"We've come this far," I murmured to Mouse. "We simply *have* to find a way in."

Mouse wasn't listening. My spaniel was squirming with sudden excitement, her short curly tail beating a quick *thump thump thump* rhythm against me. That could mean only one thing: Food must be close.

- ASIDE -

> An **aside** is when an actor onstage turns directly to the audience to make an observation or remark the rest of the actors can't hear.

Here, dear reader of the future, I pause for a moment to address you "on the side."

In the event you *did* skip the prologue (*tsk-tsk!*), I simply wish to inform you that before the Globe Theatre was built in 1599 (thanks, in part, to the gentleman Mouse and I were about to meet), the courtyards of

London inns were sometimes transformed into outdoor playhouses, especially in fair weather.

It was a cheap, exciting form of entertainment. Dramas and comedies allowed people to forget their troubles for a few hours. Queen Elizabeth herself loved the theater and it flourished during her reign. I suppose I have the queen to thank for my own love of theatricals. Some of my earliest memories were watching plays at court.

I wonder if actors will still perform outside in years to come. Though I do think a roof is rather helpful in winter.

Woof! Woooooo! Mousekin struggled in my arms. I followed her gaze. A young man, probably no older than eighteen, was grinning at Mouse. Mousekin couldn't take her eyes off him. Instantly I saw why. He held out a morsel of spiced cake: gingerbread, her favorite.

The stranger had a lean face with a high forehead. I was struck most by his bright, intelligent eyes, which seemed to laugh at everything around him—especially Mousekin. He raised an eyebrow in a question to me.

I nodded. "Yes, she may have the treat, thank you very much. But be careful of your fingers, sir." To my dog, I added a firm warning, "Mouse, be gentle. Don't snap."

Delicately, Mouse took the gingerbread with tiny white

teeth. The young man laughed and said in a low voice, "I overheard your predicament just now, mistress. If Mouse here can be silent and you don't want to miss the prologue, come along with me. I know a way to the best free seats in the house."

Mistress? Oh, pooh! I'd been found out.

"But . . . but how . . . how did you guess?" I sputtered.

"It's plain to see you've donned a disguise." The stranger grinned and pointed at my head. "Also, your curls seem to be escaping your cap in a cascade."

Frantically I began tucking my hair up. This day was *not* going as I imagined.

"I'm Will Shakespeare, an aspiring actor and a fellow theater lover," said the young man. He doffed his hat and bowed. "My father is a respectable glove maker in Stratford. I walked six days to London to make the acquaintance of this company of players and study their craft."

Should I accept his invitation? I studied him. Will Shakespeare appeared to be just as he claimed, a trustworthy young gentleman from the countryside. His clothes were simple but well kept. His boots looked muddy, muddier even than mine now were. But it was the ink that decided me.

When he'd reached out to give Mousekin her treat, I noticed his fingers were covered with smudges of ink. I held out one hand. "Along with the theater, it seems we

Deborah Hopkinson

may have something else in common, Master Shakespeare: a love of writing."

"Yes, indeed. Though I notice some of your fingers have calluses too," Will said. "Are you perchance also a musician?"

"Aye, I play the lute. I'm Emilia Bassano," I told him. "My father and his brothers came from Italy years ago to be court musicians for King Henry. Papa and his brothers are gone now, but several of my cousins still serve Queen Elizabeth; I perform with them sometimes.

"I fell in love with the theater seeing plays at the palace when I was just a little girl. I've dreamed of visiting a courtyard playhouse for a long time," I told him. "Now I'm finally here. So, yes indeed, Mouse and I will be delighted to accept your kind invitation."

"The theater captures you and doesn't let go, doesn't it? I became fascinated the very first time I saw traveling players in my village." Will Shakespeare grinned and gave Mouse the last bite of his gingerbread. "So, then, theater lovers, follow me! If we make haste, we'll be in time for the prologue."

- ASIDE -

Now, dear reader, if you recall the prologue (I told you it was useful), you already know that my new

The Plot to Kill a Queen

Thanks to Mouse, I met
Will Shakespeare of Stratford.

acquaintance did indeed go on to become a playwright, a rather remarkable one at that.

But what you may not know is that Will Shakespeare put several characters dressed in disguise into his plays, especially women disguised as men. You can find them in plays such as *Two Gentlemen of Verona*, *Twelfth Night*, *As You Like It*, and *The Merchant of Venice*.

I've often wondered if meeting me in disguise at the Bell Savage Inn that day gave him the idea. It certainly could have happened that way, don't you think? I mean, why not?

Three

 Act I, Scene 4, Interior of the Bell Savage Inn

Will Shakespeare opened a rear door of the inn and led the way up a musty wooden staircase. On the landing, he turned and put a long finger to his lips.

"We'll go out here, slink along the corridor, and then climb to the attic," he whispered with a sly grin. "It's probably best if the inn's guests don't spot riffraff like us roaming the hallways."

I smiled back and lifted one of Mouse's silky ears. "Be as quiet as your name, little one. We're having an adventure."

We tiptoed along that corridor before ducking into another stairwell. At the top, we found ourselves in a small attic space tucked in under the steep roof. It was little

The Plot to Kill a Queen

larger than a cupboard, dusty and crammed with a curious assortment of abandoned objects: traveling trunks, candlesticks, chairs with broken backs, and some old wooden toy soldiers in a broken basket.

In one corner I spied an ornate birdcage, which made me wonder if someone's poor feathered friend had found the coach journey too much. But that canary would have traveled farther than I ever had—I'd never been out of London.

Will pointed to a wooden bench in front of a window overlooking the courtyard. "After you, Mistress Bassano. Take care you don't trip on those old chipped chamber pots."

Mouse and I went to the Bell Savage Inn to see a play.

Will opened the window, and noisy chatter floated up. I could see everything! "These *are* good seats," I breathed. "I'm guessing you've been here before."

"Several times." He scanned the plain stage and the crowd below us. His eyes made me think of a quick, alert fox. "I like this vantage point. From here I can watch the audience fall into the story. I try to notice which lines make people laugh, which actors make them yawn, and which performers have people straining to catch the next words."

I leaned forward, my heart beating fast. I was here at last! I felt so excited I could barely breathe.

"Oh, look, it's starting," I whispered.

An actor walked onstage to begin the prologue. The crowd hushed. His words floated on the air, filling the space and becoming not just words, but a real story. It was as if a wizard had appeared and waved a wand. And through the actors onstage, we were magically transported to another place and time.

When Will spoke again, I'd almost forgotten where I was, or even that he was beside me. "Well, from your rapt expression, I'd say you enjoyed that very much, Mistress Bassano."

"Oh, do call me Emilia. And yes, I loved it so, so much. I loved the dramatic speeches and how the hero wooed his love. And I liked the sword fights!" I looked down and laughed.

The stage was empty. There were no sets and few props, so we used our imaginations. All the parts were played by white men, something I certainly hope has changed in your time!

"Though I'm afraid it put Mouse to sleep. Perhaps people laughing at a comedy would've helped her stay awake."

He grinned. "I did hear her snoring at one point."

I put my elbows on the sill to watch the crowd begin to stream out of the courtyard. I didn't want the magic to end. "Girls and women aren't allowed to be actors. But even if I had the chance to be onstage, I think I'd rather write a play. What a feeling it would be to see the vision from my mind become such magic, to see my words make people laugh or cry."

Beside me, Will nodded. "I feel the same."

"I'm not very good at embroidery, but it seems to me creating a play is like creating an elaborate embroidered scene," I told him. "Each stitch, like each line of dialogue, is so tiny it might not seem to matter. But when you stand back to examine the whole, all the stitches must work together, or the scene you have conjured won't make sense. You might have a bird with a twisted wing, or a tree floating above the ground."

"Well said, Emilia, and once again, I agree," Will laughed. "Our minds seem to be streams that follow the same channels. I've done a bit of acting myself and find I am annoyed when my character's lines don't make sense, or when scenes aren't stitched together properly."

"Yes, like stitches, each word counts." I looked at him curiously. "And so do you hope to act—and write plays too?"

"Yes, I'm determined to do both, though not right away. I start home for Stratford tomorrow; I'm not sure when I'll be back." He paused, his eyes on the men already dismantling the wooden stage. "I'm to be married this autumn. I hope to return someday and work in the theater to support my family."

He turned his slightly amused gaze on me. "What

about you? It is clear you have a passion for writing and the theater. Will you write a play someday for the enjoyment of your friends and family?"

I hesitated. Did I dare reveal the truth?

I hadn't told Horace or Fannie yet, and wasn't even sure I would. What if they laughed? But maybe... maybe if I shared this goal with someone, even this stranger, then my plan would feel more real. Maybe it would give me courage to actually *do* it.

"Aye, I do want to write a play. And not someday, but soon, very soon," I told Will. "That's the reason why I had to come today—to gather ideas, to experience a real playhouse for myself. But... but the script I want to write won't be just for friends and family. At least, it might not."

Will cocked his head. "What do you mean?"

"Last week, the Master of the Revels—he's in charge of entertainment at the palace—announced a royal playwriting competition." I took in a long breath. "As soon as I heard the announcement, I just knew I had to try. You may laugh, but I've made up my mind to enter it."

"A royal contest?" Will's eyebrows shot up.

"Yes! Plays must be submitted to the office of the Master of the Revels by Queene's Day, November seventeenth, the anniversary of her ascension to the throne," I explained. "It's a special contest in honor of the beginning of her twenty-fifth year as queen. The Master of the Revels will choose a winning play, which will be performed at court by young actors during the Christmas holidays."

"That sounds like a splendid idea," said Will. "Why would I laugh?"

"I've never written a play before," I said uncertainly. "I'm not even sure I can. That's why I haven't even told my two best friends."

"There's nothing lost in trying. Besides, I'll be busy in Stratford and won't be able to enter, so your field of competition is clear," Will teased. Then he frowned, struck by a thought. "But, say, will the Master of the Revels accept the work of a female playwright?"

"I . . . I'm not sure. Probably not. I think I'd better put some false name on my script," I told Will. "Though it does make me angry that a girl can't write, or act, or go to college. After all, we have a woman as queen.

"And before England was England, seven hundred years ago, Aethelflaed was the warrior queen of the region of Mercia," I went on, my words rushing out. "So why can't females—or anyone who wants to—act onstage or write plays?"

"Hear! Hear! Why not, indeed?" Will rose, and we began to make our way out of the attic.

I sighed as I stepped over some old boards. "Maybe

it's simply a foolish dream. My friend Horace says I often rush into things without stopping to think. And he may be right: I don't even have a plot."

"Why not write about her?"

"Who?"

"Aethelflaed, Lady of the Mercians," said Will. "I think we should have more plays about history, to help people imagine the past. I'd like to write such plays myself someday."

"Aethelflaed. That's a good idea." I turned the idea over in my mind. "The children of courtiers will see the play, so it would be best to write about Aethelflaed as a child—without too many bloody battles with the Vikings. I wonder if there's an old story from that time . . ."

Will and I burst out at the same time: "King Alfred and the cakes!"

"It's perfect!" I cried, laughing. "Everyone knows the old tale of how King Alfred, hiding from the Vikings, was scolded by a village woman for letting her oatcakes burn. It's probably not true, but that doesn't matter. I can imagine it in my own way and give Princess Aethelflaed a leading role."

I began to create the scenes in my head. I could envision it so clearly! The play would begin as King Alfred of Wessex, his family, and his followers celebrated Twelfth Night. Then the Danish Vikings launched a surprise attack. The Saxons of Wessex had to flee through a winter night, trudging through snow and ice to hide in the marshlands. Princess Aethelflaed and her little brother, Prince Edward, were cold and weary...

All at once I tripped. Will put out a hand to steady me and grinned. "Perhaps you should get home safely before you transport yourself to the time of the Vikings."

We were in the courtyard now and Will gestured toward the road. "Would you like me to accompany you?"

"Oh, no thank you. Mouse and I will be fine. Besides, you have a long walk before you tomorrow." I dipped a polite curtsy. "But I do thank you, sir, for a wonderful afternoon—I don't think I shall ever forget it. I'll watch for you on the London stage someday and look for plays by the celebrated William Shakespeare."

Will bowed and gave Mouse a gentle goodbye pat. Then he leaned forward, whispered something in my ear, and strode off confidently through the thinning crowd. I stood looking after him. I had a feeling Will Shakespeare would be back: Surely anyone willing to walk six days for the love of theater wouldn't give up easily.

It was at that moment that I heard a familiar name. My breath caught; I concentrated hard on listening.

"Sir Francis Walsingham thinks he's so clever," the man was saying. "Not this time."

Four

 Act I, Scene 5, Courtyard of the Bell Savage Inn

Walsingham. Sir Francis Walsingham, Queen Elizabeth's spymaster. *Why were these men talking about my guardian?*

I put Mouse down so she could sniff for crumbs. Meanwhile, I bent low, pretending to adjust my boot, keeping my face averted while I tried to see who had spoken.

I spotted them right away: two men huddled together. Their backs were toward me so I couldn't see their faces. They were well dressed. Two prosperous gentlemen, then.

Of course, I told myself, they could be talking about any number of things. After all, Sir Francis Walsingham was England's secretary of state and a public figure, one of the most powerful men in the country. These gentlemen could be discussing foreign policy or business—perhaps something to do with land or a trading ship.

Still. There was something furtive about the way they stood, heads together. I moved a little closer, then bent down again, pretending to fiddle with my other boot. I held my breath to hear better. One man seemed to be doing most of the talking.

"Now's the time," I heard him murmur. I managed to catch a few other words: "queen," "our plan." Then I heard a phrase that sent chills up my spine: "Kill the imposter."

The other man asked a question I couldn't make out. I heard one word in the answer: "Sheffield."

Sheffield. Sheffield Castle.

I'd learned this much living with the Walsingham family: Mary, Queen of Scots, was kept prisoner at Sheffield, an old medieval castle in southern Yorkshire, a few days' journey north of London. Years ago, Protestants had forced Mary, who was Catholic, off her throne in Scotland.

Mary had fled to England seeking Elizabeth's protection since the two queens were cousins. Mary hoped Elizabeth might help her regain the Scottish throne. That hadn't happened. Instead, Mary had been held prisoner for the last fourteen years.

Fannie told me her father spent hours on what she called "the Mary threat."

"Why is Mary such a threat if she's held in captivity?" I'd asked once. "Elizabeth's reign is stable. The people of England support her."

"True. But even after all this time, Mary's Catholic followers in England, as well as in France and Spain, still believe Mary also has a strong claim to be Queen of England and Ireland—a claim even stronger than Elizabeth's."

"How can that be?" I asked. "Wasn't King Henry Elizabeth's father?"

"Yes, but he was also Mary's great-uncle. The problem lies with the marriage of Elizabeth's parents. King Henry wanted to divorce his first wife to marry Anne Boleyn, Elizabeth's mother," Fannie explained. "Since the Catholic Church doesn't allow divorce, Henry left to start his own church and became a Protestant."

"So to Catholics who don't allow divorce, the marriage of Elizabeth's parents was never legal?" I asked.

"Yes, that's why they believe Mary's claim has merit," Fannie told me. "Father worries that Mary's supporters will try to kill Elizabeth and persuade the powerful Catholic countries of France and Spain to raise an army for Mary and invade England.

"That's why Father investigates any and all plots against Elizabeth."

Plots just like the one these two men seemed to be hatching. I had to get closer.

※

"Over here, Mouse," I whispered.

Fortunately, Mousekin obeyed, trotting at my heels and still eagerly sniffing the ground for crumbs. I moved to a corner, slipping behind a coach with a broken wheel. I could hear much better from here, though I didn't dare poke my head up in case the men glanced in my direction. The next words I heard sent chills down my spine.

"Walsingham and his spies will never discover how we're smuggling letters in and out of Sheffield. He's foiled us in the past. Not this time. Our new method is foolproof," said the first man. "This is the moment we've waited for all these years."

The voices faded. I peeked up to see the men walking off, their backs still toward me. Oh fie! If only I'd gotten a good look at their faces. I didn't dare chase after them.

I picked up Mouse and whispered, "Oh, Mousie, I'm afraid we're going to have to tell Sir Francis about this. And that might also mean telling about being here at the playhouse.

The Plot to Kill a Queen

"We're definitely in trouble."

I'd been so sure no one would find out about my adventure. Now I worried what Sir Francis and Lady Walsingham would do when they learned their ward had been traipsing across London in disguise.

Maybe Horace had been right after all. Maybe I shouldn't have plunged ahead. Still, if I hadn't been in the courtyard to overhear these men, what then? What if *this* was the one plot that might succeed when others in the past had failed?

I had no choice. I had to tell, no matter what the consequences to me.

Because these men wanted to kill the queen.

Five

Act I, Scene 6, Interior of Whitehall Palace, late afternoon

"Where have you been, Em?" Fannie hissed, pulling me into a corner. "And what *have* you done to your gown—your entire outfit? You look as if you've been chasing a shuttlecock across a lawn in the sun."

"Um . . . Mouse and I have been out . . . walking," I finished lamely. It wasn't a complete lie. I'd spent the whole way back from Ludgate Hill thinking about my dilemma. And I'd stumbled on a possible solution. I would simply tell *what* I'd heard—but not *where* I'd heard it.

I leaned my lute against the wall and placed my leather satchel next to it. I'd stuffed my boots and boys' clothes at the bottom. I probably wouldn't get the chance to wear them again. Yet I'd loved being able to move about so freely. The fashionable outfits we wore to court required so many layers. And it was those layers Fannie was now shaking her head at.

"You were *not* just strolling around the palace grounds, Emilia," she said in a whisper, looking around to be sure no one was near. "Your bodice is crooked, and so are your petticoats, farthingale, and your gown. I hope none of the ladies-in-waiting saw you."

I shook my head. "No, I came along empty hallways." When we were at home, I could dress simply. But on days when we came to the palace, Fannie's maid helped me with the undergarments needed to make a fashionable statement at court.

- ASIDE -

I wonder what you're wearing now, dear reader of the future, and what fashion is like in your time. I can tell you that at least among the nobles and wealthy in society, people in Elizabeth's reign are *extremely* interested in fashion. You might even say obsessed!

A woman's dress for court requires elaborate layers, starting with a smock, or chemise. Some ladies wear silk stockings; then there's a waistcoat that slips over the head, followed by a pair of bodies, which wrap around and are laced either in front or back. A farthingale goes next: It's like a wide frame of whalebone covered with fabric, and your petticoats and gown go over it. There's even more, but you get the picture.

Fashion is a bit simpler for men, though some gentlemen do like to stride about in velvet doublets, wide ruffs, and hats adorned with jewels and feathers.

I wonder if getting dressed will be quite so involved in the future. I should hope not, as I prefer comfort. And as you'll see, at times I've also found it quite helpful to be able to run.

Horace was, once again, annoyingly right. I should've chosen a day for my adventure when I didn't have to perform. But then I wouldn't have seen a play, met Will Shakespeare—or overheard the plotters. And, I reminded myself, *that* was what mattered most.

I fidgeted nervously as Fannie tugged on my clothes. What should I tell her? Officially, I served as Fannie's companion when she came to court as a junior, unmarried lady-in-waiting, called a maid of honor. That usually meant both of us being at the beck and call of the queen's older, bossy ladies, but it also gave Fannie a chance to meet courtiers and attend functions.

Unofficially, Fannie was more like an older sister—and

The Plot to Kill a Queen

my best friend (along with Horace, of course). I didn't want to cause trouble for Fannie or her parents. The family had lost Fannie's seven-year-old sister, Mary, just two years ago. Everyone was still grieving, especially Lady Walsingham, who'd suffered much in her life. Her two sons from her first marriage had been killed in a gunpowder accident. Fannie and her mother both worried constantly about Sir Francis, who worked long hours and suffered from painful ailments his doctors weren't able to cure.

"Em, I can tell by your frown there's more you want to say," Fannie murmured as she tucked a stray curl up under my coif. "I'm good at reading people, remember. I'm not my father's daughter for nothing."

"Fannie, I do want to tell you," I began. "It's just . . . I'm afraid . . ."

"Afraid? Afraid of what?" Fannie grabbed my hands so I had to look straight at her. "Tell me."

I sighed. Fannie was beautiful, poised, and stylish—but that's not what people noticed first. She truly was like her father: perceptive, shrewd, and persistent, as persistent as Mousekin trying to get every last scrap of meat from a bone.

"Fannie, I overheard two men this afternoon," I whispered. "They were talking about smuggling letters in and out of Sheffield Castle. It sounded like they were hatching a plot against Queen Elizabeth."

"What?" Fannie's sharp eyes narrowed. "Were the men here, in Whitehall Palace?"

"Um . . . no, not here."

"Where, then?" Fannie demanded. At fifteen, Fannie was nearly as imposing as her father. "Emilia, where were you?"

I hesitated. In the end, I simply couldn't lie to my best friend. "Fannie, don't be angry, but I was . . . I was at a playhouse."

"A playhouse?" Fannie stepped back in shock. "An inn playhouse?"

"I was quite safe! And I didn't stand to watch the play in the midst of a rowdy, jostling crowd," I added quickly. "I made sure no one would know it was me. I disguised myself as a servant lad."

"You went in disguise?" Frances's large, dark eyes bored into me. "Well, that explains the state of your clothes. But why go to such a place at all? We see plays at court at the holidays. Isn't that enough?"

I sighed. Will Shakespeare hadn't laughed at my plan. If a stranger didn't think it was foolish, maybe Fannie wouldn't either. On the other hand, I couldn't imagine Sir Francis would approve of his ward entering a playwriting competition, even using a false name.

"Fannie, I'll tell you precisely why I went there today.

But it would be best if it stayed our secret," I began. "Will you promise?"

She turned this over a moment. At last she said, "You had better tell me first."

"Do you remember the announcement last week about the play contest?" I asked. I didn't wait for her answer. "I intend to enter. But it's been ages since I've seen a play. So I simply *had* to go to a playhouse today: to get ideas and inspiration. And I did!

"Not that I'll win, of course," I added hastily. "But, Fannie, you know how much I love seeing plays. And you see how many candles I've used staying up late writing down the stories that come into my head. This is my chance to prove to myself I can write a real play—an entire play from beginning to end, with characters, scenes, dialogue, and a plot. Please understand. I just have to try."

Fannie said nothing (which was unusual, since she had an opinion on everything). She had a dazed expression on her face, as if I were speaking in a language she didn't know.

"Anyway, all that isn't important right now," I continued, waving a hand in the air. "What matters, Fannie, is that after the play I overheard those suspicious-sounding gentlemen. So what do you think? Is this plot something your father should be told about?"

Fannie seemed not to have heard me. She shook her

head. "I can't believe you went to a play. In disguise. Did no one suspect you were a girl?"

"No! Well, just one person, but he only cared about the play too, and thanks to him, I was able to watch from the inn, rather than standing in the courtyard," I told her. "But what about the men? Do we need to tell your father?"

"Of course we must," Fannie said matter-of-factly. "Father says his intelligence work is like a painting. Close up, each brushstroke might not make sense. But if you step back, the whole is revealed. He focuses on each brushstroke, however small."

I nodded. It was similar to what Will Shakespeare and I had talked about just a few hours before. Just as with writing a play or designing an elaborate panel of embroidery, each tiny detail mattered to Sir Francis. And in this case, the details—even the conversation I happened to overhear—could help him better protect the queen.

"Fannie, could you maybe mention this to your father first—before I have to talk to him?" I pleaded. "I wish you didn't have to tell him where I was. I love living with your family. I'm afraid he'll be so angry he'll make me leave."

"I don't think it will come to that, Em. After all, my father made a promise to your papa. I will try to smooth the waters, but you should be prepared for a fierce scolding," she warned.

"Oh, thank you, Fannie. And, please don't tell him about the competition," I asked. "I won't use my own name to enter: No one will ever know."

I grabbed her hands, which were arranging curls around my forehead. "It's not as if I have much chance of winning—I am sure there will be real playwrights who enter. But I have my heart set on trying to do this. Besides, I don't think it's fair that girls aren't allowed to do things like act onstage or go to college."

Unequal education, I knew, was something Fannie *did* care about passionately.

"No, it certainly isn't fair," she agreed. "Father went to college and then studied at Gray's Inn to qualify as a lawyer. Elizabeth is the Patron Lady of Gray's Inn, but no one even considers allowing women to enter the profession. So I won't be able to follow in my father's footsteps."

"Yet you'd be an excellent lawyer, Fannie, and a remarkable secretary of state," I said. "And so . . . about the competition . . . ?"

"All right, I concede that point: I won't mention the contest," Fannie relented. "But I *will* have to tell Father that you visited a playhouse. I'll simply say you love the theater so much you impulsively decided to attend.

"I do have a condition, though," she added, a smile playing on her lips. "You must let me read your script when it's done."

"I'll do better than that. If I can complete a script, we can perform it together. I'll get Horace to play a part too," I said. "You shall be the heroine."

Fannie, I thought, would make an excellent Princess Aethelflaed. Horace could be King Alfred. I could play the villager who bakes the cakes. Maybe I'd also take on the role of Guthrum, king of the Danish Vikings. I mean, if men can play women's parts onstage, why not?

Just then, we heard laughter and the rustle of ladies' gowns at the far end of the corridor. The musicians would be gathering soon on the Minstrels' Balcony.

"It's time. You look perfectly tidy now, Emilia, at least for a few minutes," Fannie said wryly. "I'm sure Her Majesty

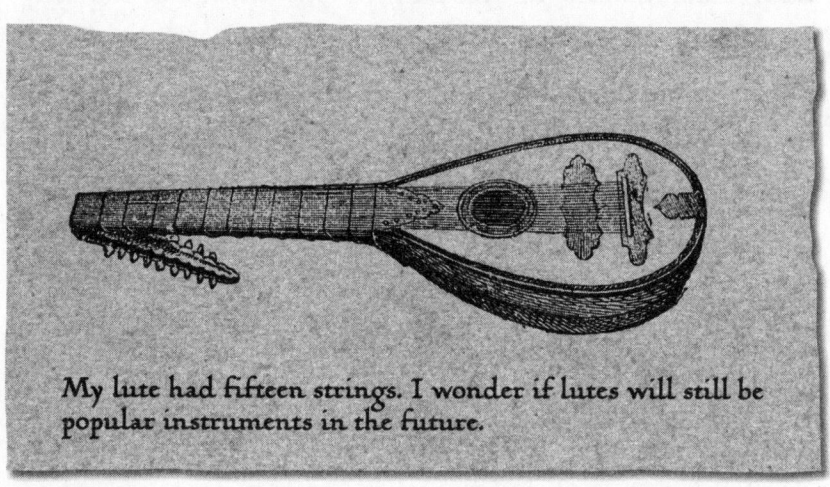

My lute had fifteen strings. I wonder if lutes will still be popular instruments in the future.

will be delighted when she looks up from the Great Hall and spots her favorite lute player."

"I'm not her favorite," I protested. "Also, I won't be long, so perhaps you can wait for me. Cousin Arthur has asked me to perform only one song, 'Greensleeves.'"

"Mouse and I will wait, and then we can go home by the river. Mother has sent a servant to accompany us." Fannie scooped up Mouse and my satchel.

"Fannie . . ." I picked up my lute and hesitated. "Thank you. I'm so glad you're my friend."

I could still remember the day Sir Francis had come to visit, when Papa was so sick. After Sir Francis left, Papa had taken my hand. "When I'm gone, my dear, Sir Francis and Lady Walsingham will care for you."

"Papa, I don't even know them!"

"You'll come to know them, Emilia. Their older daughter, Frances, is about your age. Sir Francis is powerful and influential. As his ward, you'll receive an education and make a fine match someday. Your Bassano cousins will always be there to support you, but they can't give you the same opportunities."

"I only want you to get well, Papa," I cried. "And I don't understand . . . If Sir Francis is so important, why would he be willing to help us?"

"Sir Francis does this for me," Papa said softly. "That is all you need to know, Emilia."

Sometimes I wish I'd asked Papa more questions, but I was only seven that spring. I'd lived with the Walsinghams for six years now. Fannie could have looked down her nose at me—the poor daughter of an immigrant musician. She never had.

Now, as I started to scurry off, Fannie called, "Don't forget the words of your song, Em."

"I know 'Greensleeves' by heart," I reminded her. "It's the first song Papa taught me."

I could almost hear Papa's gentle voice, "Even when you know a song by heart, keep practicing. There is always room for practice."

And so I sang softly under my breath as I hurried to join the other musicians.

Alas, my love, you do me wrong
To cast me off discourteously.
For I have loved you well and long
Delighting in your company.
Greensleeves was all my joy
Greensleeves was my delight,
Greensleeves was my heart of gold,
And who but my Lady Greensleeves.

The Plot to Kill a Queen

Later, from the musicians' gallery above the hall, I could see the queen among her guests. Elizabeth looked magnificent in a bright white gown festooned with colorful shimmering threads.

When the last note of my song faded, Her Majesty gazed right at me and inclined her head.

My eyes filled with tears. I had pleased a queen, but in my heart I sang for Papa.

Six

Act I, Scene 7, Walsingham home on Seething Lane, London, later that evening

"Mistress Bassano, isn't it?" asked the clerk. "Sir Francis wishes to see you in his study."

I'd just come in from taking Mouse out for a walk when Thomas Phillips stopped me in the hall. Clerks and officials were always coming and going at the Walsingham's large house on Seething Lane. I didn't know most of their names. But we all knew Thomas, Sir Francis's special assistant, who never seemed to leave.

"Whenever I pass Thomas, he looks through me as if I'm not there," I'd told Fannie once.

Fannie had laughed. "Oh, that's because his head is

full of secret codes. Father says Thomas is a genius at languages. No one can create a cipher to fool him. He helps Father decipher intercepted letters to or from the Scots queen."

Thomas was still staring, his unkempt hair spilling over one eye. He frowned, as if trying to recall what else he had meant to say. Then he glanced down at Mouse, who wagged her tail and fixed him with hopeful brown eyes. *No chance of a treat from him*, I wanted to tell her.

"Sir Francis expects you immediately, so you may as well bring . . . that creature," Thomas said, wrinkling his nose in distaste. "Don't let it loose. There are *immensely* important papers in his office."

I wanted to argue that Mouse hadn't torn up paper since she was a puppy, but instead I just bobbed a polite

This is a portrait of Fannie's father, Sir Francis Walsingham, the queen's spymaster. I was a little afraid of him. Can you see why?

curtsy. Not that Thomas noticed. He was already scuttling off, moving so quickly the hall candles flickered in their sconces. I walked slowly to the end of the hall and stopped before the large wooden door.

"Be good, Mousekin," I whispered, swallowing hard. "No yapping at Sir Francis."

I rapped and a muffled voice responded, "Enter."

I entered and curtsied. "You asked to see me, Sir Francis."

"Ah yes, I'll be with you in a moment, Emilia," Sir Francis said, without looking up from the paper before him. He waved his quill. "Please take a seat."

"Yes, sir." At first, though, I didn't move. All I could do was look around me.

I'd once asked Fannie what her father did in his study from morning until late at night.

"Everything for England," she'd said. "That's partly why he rarely dines with us and why Mother worries so about his health. Even when he is exhausted and in pain, Father never stops. He writes letters; he drafts policies and treaties. Most of all, he tries to protect Elizabeth and keep England at peace."

Everything for England. And here it was. Rows of chests stood open, maps and masses of paper spilling out. Against the walls, shelves of thick, leather-bound books stretched floor to ceiling. As I scanned the shelves, I wondered if even one of these books had been written by a woman. I imagined not.

I will finish my play, I vowed. *And when I grow up, I'll write a book. Maybe I'll even start a school for girls.* I knew I probably couldn't single-handedly make universities accept female students or open up the theater or the profession of law to women. I couldn't change all of society. But I could do something small—something with my own life.

It would be like chipping away at a great stone wall with a tiny blade. Still, after I was gone, the blade would be there for someone else to pick up to keep chipping away. And then I imagined others joining in, until the wall crumbled to dust in a time too far in the future for me to see.

"Emilia? Shall we begin?" Sir Francis's voice startled me from my wandering thoughts.

I moved forward to perch on the edge of a massive wooden chair. I had sat in this same chair, my toes not touching the floor, the first time I'd come here after Papa died. I don't think I noticed the books and the chests of papers then. I was too frightened, my eyes blurry with tears.

I'd been scared of Sir Francis, but he'd been surprisingly kind. He spoke gently, telling me how much he'd admired Papa and his music, and that he and Lady Walsingham hoped I would be content living with their family.

But now. Now I feared Sir Francis would tell me my conduct was disgraceful—so disgraceful it would be best if I stayed with my cousin Arthur.

I settled Mouse on my lap and took a breath, my heart pounding. I knew Fannie had pulled her father aside after supper. Fannie had kept her promise: She hadn't mentioned the play contest. But she had told Sir Francis I'd gone to an inn playhouse, where I'd overheard a suspicious conversation.

I gazed over the enormous black desk to find Sir Francis studying me. I steeled myself for the worst, expecting Sir Francis to issue a stern rebuke for flaunting the conduct expected of young ladies, noble or not.

If Will Shakespeare had reminded me of a bright, sly fox, Sir Francis was more like an old, experienced hawk, a hunter who'd learned to practice patience. It was easy to imagine him, alert and still, just waiting for his prey to make a false move.

And that's exactly what I'd done: made a false move. I'd spent six years under this roof as a grateful, compliant ward. In one day, I'd let loose my true rebellious nature. Like a small mouse, I'd lost patience hiding in my hole. My hunger for excitement, for drama, had made me take risks. I'd broken free. Now I'd been caught.

So when Sir Francis spoke at last, his first words took

The Plot to Kill a Queen

me by complete surprise. "Emilia, Her Majesty was quite pleased with your performance earlier this evening."

"Um . . . oh, thank you, sir." I felt confused. *What? How does Sir Frances even know this? And why mention it now?*

Sir Francis smiled, noticing my confusion. "I met with the queen briefly after your performance to get some papers signed. She's aware you're my ward and remarked that you have the spirit of your father, whom she remembers fondly, as do I. He was a bright spirit at court and served his queen well."

I felt my eyes fill with tears. "Sir Francis, I want to say how grateful I am for all you and Lady Walsingham have done for me. I'm . . . I'm sorry about my conduct earlier today. I got . . . carried away."

Sir Francis steepled his fingers and fixed me with a piercing stare. "Ah, yes, about that. I understand you attended a play at the Bell Savage Inn on Ludgate Hill."

"Yes, sir." I lowered my eyes to stare at the top of Mouse's soft brown fur.

But wait. How did Sir Francis know exactly where I'd gone? I hadn't mentioned the name of the playhouse to Fannie. True, the Bell Savage was the most popular inn playhouse. Yet I might have gone to another inn, like the Cross Keys on Gracechurch Street.

Maybe Horace was right. Maybe Sir Francis really did have spies everywhere.

"Fannie mentioned you overheard two men there," he prompted.

"Yes, sir." I repeated what I'd heard, trying to remember each detail. At the end, I said, "Sir, they did seem sure their new method of smuggling letters in and out of Sheffield Castle wouldn't be discovered. They said it was foolproof."

I paused. "Could it be a serious plot against our queen?"

"Possibly," he said. "I cannot say until we know more. Some plots are frivolous, concocted by those who have romantic notions of saving Mary. Yet even these must be investigated.

"I take all plots seriously," Sir Francis continued. "There's always the chance Mary's Catholic followers here will be able to rally strong support in France or Spain for her cause—enough support to raise an army to rescue her. Those powerful Catholic countries would be glad for an excuse to invade England and would prefer a Catholic monarch to our current Protestant queen."

An invasion. I thought of Princess Aethelflaed, fleeing from Viking invasions as a child seven hundred years ago. What would it be like, to have your homeland overtaken and the peace destroyed? If that happened, innocent people would surely suffer.

"And so you will investigate what the men were saying?" I asked.

"Yes, which brings us back to you, Emilia."

"Me, sir?"

"It's clear something is going on at Sheffield Castle that my intelligence gatherers there haven't discovered. Or perhaps my agents have been turned to the other side. I cannot say. I do know we must act quickly," Sir Francis said, his voice now low and intense.

"Some people might consider my methods of gathering intelligence a bit unusual," he went on. "But this information, along with Queen Elizabeth's praise for you this evening, has put a notion into my head of how to proceed."

"I'm not sure I understand, Sir Francis." I didn't understand at all, in fact.

"There are no rules in this game," said Sir Francis, rubbing his brow as though his head ached. "I must always ask myself, 'Who is best placed to find out what plots are brewing? How can I make a move our enemies will never suspect—or anticipate?'

"And that's where you come in, Emilia. I don't approve of your escapade today. I trust it will never happen again.

However, it shows you are creative and bold—qualities I look for in those who do this work for the realm. These are the very qualities that make a good agent."

A good agent! I stared. What was Sir Francis talking about?

"Emilia, if you're willing, I'd like you to undertake a mission for me—or rather, for your queen," Sir Francis said.

I swallowed hard. "Um...what...what would I need to do?"

"It's a sound plan, I think. Elizabeth is an accomplished musician and patron of the arts. Mary is fond of young people and eager for any gesture of kindness from her cousin," he told me. "So what would be more natural than for Elizabeth to send a talented young lute player on a visit to Sheffield to entertain her cousin for several weeks?"

I swallowed hard as his meaning sank in. "Are you saying, sir, that you wish me to go to Sheffield Castle, to where Mary, Queen of Scots, is held captive?"

"That's it. You needn't worry, Emilia. You'll be quite safe. But we must find out how letters are being smuggled in and out of the castle. My agents there have told me nothing, which is worrisome. Double agents abound in this business."

Sir Francis leaned forward, his voice still low, though no one else was near. "I'd like you to be my eyes and ears on the ground, Emilia. Look around, see what you can discover. Listen to servants; watch Mary's staff and her ladies-in-waiting."

"Sir Francis, I doubt Mary's ladies will talk to me," I said, thinking of the arrogant, snobbish ladies at Elizabeth's court. "They'll see me as beneath them."

"That may be, but you can still observe them. And there is one young lady in particular I'd like you to get to know: Bessie Pierrepont. She's a favorite of the Scots queen. Bessie is Fannie's age, about fifteen. Her grandmother is Bess of Hardwick, the current wife of Mary's jailer, the Earl of Shrewsbury, who owns Sheffield Castle."

"Do you suspect Bessie of being a traitor, sir?"

He considered this a moment, then shook his head. "I doubt it. However, she is close to Mary. She'll be aware of the queen's moods and who has Mary's ear."

"Why would Bessie tell me anything?"

He smiled. "She may not. Not directly. But talking to her might give you insights. For instance, Bessie may be peeved if Mary ignores her and instead is huddled with one of her secretaries writing letters. Also, if Mary is in excellent spirits, that may be a sign the plot is progressing and Mary thinks freedom is close."

I nodded slowly. "I . . . think I could do something like that—watch and listen." Though I thought Fannie, with her exceptional ability to read people, would be a lot better at it. "How long would I stay at the castle?"

As I asked the question my mind was racing. What about my play? Scripts had to be turned into the Office of Revels by November seventeenth, the anniversary of the queen's ascension to the throne. Would I have to give up my goal of entering the contest?

"Perhaps a month or so," Sir Francis said. "I'll draft a letter from Elizabeth to Andrew Melville, who runs Mary's household, to inform him of your visit. It's best to keep my name out of it. We will only mention your Bassano connections. No sense in bringing light to the fact that you're my ward.

"Also, we are in luck. A friend named ... uh, Mrs. Hughes, who has done good turns for us in the past, paid me a visit this evening. Mrs. Hughes is heading to Sheffield herself, the day after tomorrow. It's a three-day journey and she's willing to be your chaperone," said Sir Francis. "She'll be a great help to you in this undertaking."

He glanced down at notes he had made. "I believe that's all for now. We can talk again tomorrow. Lady Walsingham will help you pack and ensure you have suitable gowns and warm clothes. It's said to be a rather damp, cold place."

Sir Francis looked up and must have noticed the blank

expression on my face. "Forgive me; I'm accustomed to acting at once when the need is urgent. Perhaps I have been too hasty. If you do not wish to go, Emilia, obviously we will say no more about it."

I was silent, turning over his extraordinary request in my mind. Sir Francis didn't want me to leave his family. Quite the opposite: He believed I was capable of being one of his agents. He'd even begun preparations.

And all along, Sir Francis had guessed I wouldn't refuse this challenge.

"Yes, I will go and do my best," I told the queen's spymaster. I paused, my hand on Mousekin's soft head. "I do have one question, though."

"Certainly, my dear. What is it?"

"Just this, sir." I smiled. "May I bring my dog?"

※

"Father is sending you to Sheffield Castle alone?" Fannie exclaimed when I returned to our bedchamber. She sat before her mirror, and with every word combed her long hair with a harder stroke.

"Not entirely. Your father said I'm to have a chaperone called Mrs. Hughes. The journey takes three days; I suppose that means we'll stay in coaching inns for two nights,"

I told her. "I've never stayed at an inn. I've never even been out of London."

"And then what?" Fannie demanded. "Will this Mrs. Hughes remain with you in that wretched old medieval castle with those horrid people?"

"Um, well, he said Mrs. Hughes would be a great help to me in this undertaking. So I assume she'll stay."

I frowned, trying to remember exactly what Sir Francis had said. As it turned out, I'd had additional questions, and Sir Francis and I had spoken for several minutes more, but now my mind was spinning too fast to recall every detail.

"I wish *you* could come, Fannie, though I know that wouldn't be wise. Sir Francis told me not to mention my connection to him," I went on.

I paced across the room, unable to sit still. Mouse stretched out on the bed and watched me curiously. "I am to say I live with my Bassano cousins. Otherwise, people will suspect me of being . . ."

"One of Sir Francis Walsingham's spies," Fannie finished. "Father might use the words *reporters* or *agents* to describe his helpers, but he is well known as Elizabeth's spymaster."

"So that's why you can't come, I suppose. Besides," I teased, "you probably don't wish to be parted from a brilliant poet named Philip Sidney."

The Plot to Kill a Queen

At fifteen, Fannie already had a bevy of suitors. But though Philip was more than ten years her senior, she'd made her choice. Fannie and Philip hoped to marry next year, after she turned sixteen.

"I suppose Father is right about my not going, though I wish I could meet the Scots queen," Fannie said. "You must tell me all about her. She was once thought a great beauty. She has had three husbands, you know. And the third probably murdered the second.

"There are several other reasons I can't go, aside from being the spymaster's daughter," Fannie added. "And it's not just about Philip. It's an especially busy time at court, with many foreign visitors expected."

Fannie turned in her chair and sent me a slow, steady look, as if there were some hidden meaning to her words she expected me to grasp.

Suddenly I did understand. "Fannie! Are you trying to tell me you *already* do this sort of work for your father?"

"Of course I do, Em." Fannie grinned. "I've helped Father for several years now. I thought by now you would've guessed. Why do you think I spend so much time with visitors to court, especially those from the continent?"

"Oh, and now that I think on it, Philip is often there as well, chatting right alongside you," I exclaimed. "He gathers intelligence for your father too?"

Fannie nodded. "Philip is a rising star at court and has long been a protégé of Father's. That's how we came to know each other."

"But . . . but how do you do it, Fannie?"

"It's simple really. We make light conversation, ask questions, and try to determine if people are sympathetic to the Scots queen. People like to hear themselves talk and boast about their connections and their own importance.

"Flattery is a useful tool, Em. Never underestimate the power of flattery."

I shook my head. "I had no idea."

"Your mouth is quite open." Fannie reached over to tap my nose gently with the tip of her finger. "Understand this about Father: He'll do whatever he must to keep Elizabeth safe. As I'm sure he told you, he's not afraid to use unusual methods. He has intelligence gatherers of all sorts: servants, innkeepers, merchants, all watching and listening to uncover possible intrigues."

"Well, Sir Francis even has a dog working for him now," I said, pointing at the bed where Mouse had now curled up in a furry ball and started to snore.

"By all means, bring Mouse," Sir Francis had said when I asked. "The Scots queen is quite fond of dogs and has several as pets. Perhaps your little spaniel can be helpful."

Mousekin and I were about to become spies.

The Plot to Kill a Queen

- INTERMISSION/INTERVAL -

> An **intermission** or **interval** is a break between parts of a performance. Audience members often make use of the time to go to the restroom or buy refreshments.

Dear Reader,

Since you've now met Will Shakespeare, you might be curious to know the answer to Emilia's wondering about the First Folio. This collection of thirty-six Shakespeare plays, compiled by friends seven years after the Bard's death, was published in the fall of 1623.

According to the Folger Shakespeare Library, about eighteen of Shakespeare's plays probably would have been lost completely had they not been collected and published then. In our time (the twenty-first century), 235 First Folios survive. Learn more at: www.folger.edu/shakespeare/first-folio.

Emilia was certainly correct about the cost. In July 2022, a First Folio sold at auction for $2.4 million.

If you wish to take this opportunity to get some refreshments, by all means, do so. Now back to Emilia!

Act II
The Play's the Thing

Mary, Queen of Scots.

"THE PLAY'S THE THING /
WHEREIN I'LL CATCH THE CONSCIENCE
OF THE KING."
—William Shakespeare, Hamlet,
Act II, Scene 2

Seven

🖋 **Act II, Scene 1, London, early morning, two days later**

"You'll use the name Emily Hughes on our journey," my chaperone announced as our carriage rumbled off from the Walsingham home. We were headed to the White Horse Inn on Fetter Lane. From there we'd catch the mail coach to Sheffield.

"Yes, Mrs. Hughes," I sniffed, craning my neck to wave once more at the Walsinghams, who'd all risen early to see me off. My stomach felt queasy. I was already thinking this might be another instance of my leaping ahead without thinking. Was I ready? Could I truly succeed at the mission Sir Francis had given me?

And who was this Mrs. Hughes anyway? She'd seemed to appear out of nowhere in the predawn darkness. Had she walked from somewhere close by, or perhaps spent the night in our house?

I'd finished hugging Fannie for the third time and she was planting a kiss on Mousekin's nose when I turned around, and suddenly Mrs. Hughes was simply there, conferring in low tones with Sir Francis. I was already a little afraid of her.

"You are to call me Aunt," she instructed now. "Should anyone ask, we are visiting a sick relative. However, I prefer that you leave the talking to me. At Sheffield, someone from the coaching inn will convey us to the castle. Only then may you resume your true identity.

"Are you listening, child? Are you even awake?" Mrs. Hughes barked. She wore her hair pulled back severely under a black cap and hood. She'd wrapped a muffler, or scarf, around her neck, covering the lower part of her face. She looked every bit the part of a stern widow. And perhaps that's exactly what she was.

"Yes, Mrs. Hughes, I'm awake. I'm . . . I just feel sad leaving my . . . my friends." I sniffed, wiping away tears. I hadn't been parted from Fannie since I'd come to live with her family after Papa died.

And I'd never gone anywhere alone. Well, almost alone.

Mrs. Hughes waved a hand, as if sweeping away anything to do with feelings. "Aunt. Remember, you are to call me Aunt. Starting now."

"But we're alone in this carriage! No one can hear..." I could just make out her fierce stare as the night lifted. "Yes, Aunt, I understand."

I yawned, and buried my face in Mousekin's soft fur, trying to quiet my racing heart. I'd been too excited to sleep much. Yesterday had passed in a whirlwind. Lady Walsingham and Fannie had spent the day helping me gather clothes to pack into a small trunk. Fannie insisted on lending me extra finery.

"Take this, and this, and my new russet-colored French gown, Em," she'd said, tossing items on the bed. "You must impress the Scots queen and her ladies with your London fashions."

Lady Walsingham surprised me with the gift of a fine brown woolen cloak. "You will need this for the journey, and probably in that old chilly castle too."

She'd draped it around my shoulders and kissed my forehead. "You look lovely, my dear. This light shade of brown matches your eyes."

"Thank you, Lady Walsingham." Impulsively, I hugged her, and felt her arms tighten around me.

"I know I've been distant since we lost our little Mary.

But it's a comfort to have your bright presence here, Emilia. Sir Francis is grateful to you for taking this on and I am too. As you know, these matters weigh on him so heavily," she said softly. Then she added, "Your father would be proud of the young woman you are becoming."

I'd wanted to say goodbye to Horace too, but there hadn't been time to go to Whitehall Palace. Instead, I'd scrawled a hasty message saying I'd be departing the following morning on an unexpected visit to friends of the Walsinghams.

I'd sent a similar note to my cousin Arthur, on Sir Francis's instructions. He advised, "The fewer people who know exactly where you're headed, the better."

✼

When we alighted at the White Horse Inn, I stood shivering while my trunk and Mrs. Hughes's bag were loaded onto the coach.

Mouse poked her little head up from my satchel like a tiny bird in a nest. I held the leather bag close to my chest. Even in the early morning this yard was bustling. I didn't want to take a chance of Mouse getting under horse hooves and carriage wheels.

At first, Mouse was calm, sniffing and listening, her

oval eyes wide. All at once, she started to whine. I thought someone nearby must have food.

It was even better.

"Horace! What... whatever are you doing here?" I sputtered as he strode toward us. "How did you even know I'd be here?"

"Sir Francis isn't the only one who hears things," Horace whispered. He placed a large wrapped packet into my hands. "Gingerbread and oatcakes! I got up early, snuck into the kitchens, and baked these special.

"I made extra for you, Mousie. I know how hungry you get." Horace leaned forward and planted a soft kiss on Mouse's muzzle and then one on my cheek. I wished I could tell him where I was going, but one glance at my chaperone's face made me clamp my lips tight.

"It's time to go," said Mrs. Hughes. Horace doffed his cap and helped her into the coach. "Here you go, mistress." How he could smile at this early hour I didn't know. My chaperone said nothing, but acknowledged him with a small nod.

Horace held out his hand to me. "Farewell, intrepid travelers. Be safe, Em, and try not to get into trouble. And, as always, that goes for you too, Mouse."

Then, a little louder so Mrs. Hughes could hear, for

some reason he added, "And do share my gingerbread with your kind chaperone. I have a hunch she'll enjoy it."

I waved until carts and horses blocked my view. "That young man is a friend of yours?" asked Mrs. Hughes.

"Oh, yes. Horace is an excellent cook too. The queen herself has praised his gingerbread. Wait until you taste it!" I babbled now, feeling nervous as we rolled through the streets.

"He bakes gingerbread, does he? Perhaps he got the recipe from his mother," said Mrs. Hughes, almost to herself.

I didn't answer. I wasn't even sure if Horace had parents or a family. It wasn't unusual for apprentices to leave home, but Horace always changed the subject when I asked about his past. I also didn't know if he'd been born here in London or, like Will Shakespeare and Papa, traveled far to this city to pursue a dream.

And now I was traveling too. But for a different reason. I sighed as we rumbled farther and farther away from the center of London. This whole adventure had begun with my dream of writing a play. Now that didn't seem possible. I'd hoped to borrow some money from Fannie and visit a stationer's stall for paper and writing materials. But in yesterday's swirl of activity there hadn't been time.

I'm doing something more important than entering a playwriting competition, I told myself. *Something to help the queen.*

At least, I would try to help. But was I smart and shrewd enough? Was I brave enough?

At that moment, Mousekin gave a little bark and reached her front paws up on my chest to snuggle my neck and lick my cheek.

"I know what you're after, little one," I whispered. "Horace's gingerbread for breakfast."

Mouse gobbled up her treat, then buried her head under my arm and snuggled in close with a contented sigh. Whatever happened, at least my little dog believed in me.

Act II, Scene 2, On various and sundry muddy roads heading north

"Silence, Emily! You're making my head ache," Mrs. Hughes grumbled. "I don't believe you've stopped chattering since we left London two days ago."

"Sorry, um... Aunt." I settled back on the hard seat. "There's so much to look at!"

She raised an eyebrow. "Do you mean cows, sheep, and thatched-roof cottages, the same sights we've passed hour after bumpy hour?"

"Well, yes. But the cows have such charming faces. And I love how the sheep cuddle close together, their backs to the slashing rain, to help keep one another warm," I cried.

"Mouse likes sheep too. Especially when a herd crosses the road and our coach has to stop. Don't you, Mousekin? Do you like when they say *baa baa*?"

Woo! Woo! Mouse lifted her muzzle high and yowled, her tail thumping. My little Mousekin *loved* sheep.

In truth I'd been a bit worried, but Mouse was turning out to be an excellent traveler. Except for the occasional burst of excited yapping, she'd used the time to nap or wag her tail excitedly at various farm animals.

My chaperone certainly seemed to think my spaniel was a more desirable companion than I was. Besides chattering far too much (polite young girls should stay silent, eyes lowered, unless addressed by an adult), I also kept forgetting my name was supposed to be Emily and that I was to call her aunt.

What if Mrs. Hughes decides I am completely unfit before we even reach Sheffield? I worried. *What if she determines to bring me back to London to face Sir Francis in disgrace, my mission in tatters and my queen in danger?*

I shivered and pulled my cloak close around me, staring out at rain-soaked fields. Tonight would be our last stop at an inn. From this point on, I would have to play my part better.

I risked a glance at Mrs. Hughes, bland and gray as her

traveling cloak. She said little, to me or anyone else. She seemed every bit a quiet, respectable widow.

Still, when I recalled Sir Francis and his "unusual" methods, I couldn't shake the feeling Mrs. Hughes might not be exactly what she seemed.

- ASIDE -

Our journey would have been quicker on horseback, of course. There have been improvements in transportation since my first journey. The earliest coaches had neither springs nor windows. No wonder I was sore! The roads are better now too.

༼༽

"Are we almost there?" I asked Mrs. Hughes. It was the last afternoon of our journey. And while I still enjoyed gazing out at farms, villages, and great sweeps of rolling hillsides, I was feeling very sore indeed from all the bumping and jostling. The weather had turned rainy and blustery and I was glad for Lady Walsingham's cloak.

"We'll arrive in Sheffield before dark," Mrs. Hughes told me. "Before that, we have one more stop at an inn to change horses. We're sure to pick up fellow passengers there; this is our last chance to speak alone. Please remember everything I've told you. Most especially, remember to play your part."

"Yes, Aunt," I sighed, resting my chin on the top of Mouse's head. Mrs. Hughes had used the evenings when we'd been alone in our chambers at inns to share details about the Scots queen and Sheffield Castle. How she knew these details, I didn't dare to ask.

Most of all, she'd stressed that I must play my part as a young musician, with no knowledge of Sir Francis or plots. I thought of what Will Shakespeare had said about actors, and how some seemed to become their characters. That's what I needed to do.

Today my role was still Emily, niece of Mrs. Hughes. At Sheffield Castle, I'd become Emilia again, but an innocent Emilia, asking innocent questions. I needed to be an Emilia who kept her wits about her, an Emilia who knew nothing of royal intrigue, the deadly rivalry of queens, or secret letters or plots.

I can do it. I can play that part, I told myself. As we rumbled up to a small coaching inn, I assured Mrs. Hughes, "Aunt, you can depend on me."

Mrs. Hughes nodded. "I hope so. This is not some childish game, you know. Sir Francis is counting on you."

And so was my queen.

Just as Mrs. Hughes predicted, we weren't alone for the

last leg of our journey. Two older gentlemen joined us. Mrs. Hughes greeted the newcomers briefly, then appeared to drop off to sleep, her face nearly hidden by her thick scarf. By now, though, I suspected that even when she appeared to be napping, my chaperone heard every word around her.

One gentleman was especially talkative, addressing me in a loud raspy voice, "Knives. Do you know about the knives, young lady?"

"I beg your pardon, sir?"

"Sheffield. That's what we're known for: excellent knives and cutlery," said the man. "We're known for our famous guest too. Though I suppose I should call her a prisoner.

"She's certainly a burden on George Talbot, the Earl of Shrewsbury," he went on. "They say the Scots queen and her staff are eating and drinking up all his wealth. She insists on washing and bathing in white wine!"

I thought it was only polite to say something, so I murmured, "Oh my."

"The earl does his best," he said, warming to his subject. "But what thanks does he get? They say he has to beg Elizabeth for an allowance, which doesn't begin to cover Mary's expenses. The Scots queen is supposed to be a great horsewoman, yet I imagine Talbot quakes in his boots when she goes out riding. If his precious prisoner managed to escape, Elizabeth might decide to lock *him* in the Tower and lop off his head!"

The man guffawed, as though he had made a humorous jest. Mrs. Hughes opened her eyes and spoke in a fussy, flustered sort of way. "Oh, dear sir! Surely this is not proper conversation for my niece's delicate young ears. Why, such talk makes my own heart flutter."

The man mumbled an apology. I smiled to myself. Mrs. Hughes was definitely playing a part herself. She hadn't been flustered once—not when we had to stop in a lonely section of road to repair a broken wheel, or just a little while ago, when our coach had to be pushed out of a ditch in a downpour.

The coach driver had flagged down two young men driving a sturdy farm wagon and begged their help. I'd peered to look, but couldn't see their faces since their caps were pulled down low against the heavy shower. Mrs. Hughes said stoically, "Mud or not, we may need to alight, Emily, if they cannot budge the coach."

But they had freed us. Before we started out again, Mrs. Hughes waved one of the boys over. She leaned forward, blocking my view, and pressed some coins into his hands.

"Pleased to be of service; my mum always taught me to help ladies in distress," he said cheerfully, as though he didn't mind being covered in mud.

The Plot to Kill a Queen

Mousekin and I enjoyed the coach ride though it was extremely bumpy. At one point we even had to be pushed and pulled out of the mud.

Now Mrs. Hughes turned back to the gentleman. She cleared her throat and said, "I'm sure the earl and his lady do the best they can, sir."

"Aye, you're right about that. Bess of Hardwick even spends time doing needlework with their royal prisoner. Her granddaughter Bessie Pierrepont is said to be a great favorite of the Scots queen," he said.

At that, my ears pricked up, though, following Mrs. Hughes's advice (for once), I kept my eyes lowered. Bessie was the girl Sir Francis had asked me to befriend.

"Still, it's been a drain," the portly gentleman continued. "And I'm sure the earl would not blink an eye if a certain queen was parted with her head, if you get my meaning. Solve his problem now, wouldn't it?"

"Sir, I must again beseech you to watch your tongue," Mrs. Hughes reminded him. But when I stole a glance, I saw she was biting her lip to keep from smiling.

If the servants at Sheffield Castle gossiped as freely as this gentleman, perhaps my task wouldn't be so hard.

Eight

Act II, Scene 3, Courtyard of the Rose and Crown coaching inn in Sheffield

At last! It felt good to have my feet on solid ground. I drew in a deep breath of crisp air. The late afternoon sky had cleared; the brisk breeze a reminder it was now October. By the time I left Yorkshire, trees would be shaking off their leaves.

"We'll meet our cart around back," said Mrs. Hughes, leading the way to the rear of the Rose and Crown. Mousekin whined and I let her out of the satchel so she could relieve herself under a bush.

"I imagine you're hungry, Mouse," I said, scooping her up again. "I am too, but 'Aunt' says there isn't time."

I rejoined Mrs. Hughes, who still had her scarf pulled up over the lower part of her face; I imagined she didn't like the wind, though it crossed my mind that, for some reason, she didn't want to be seen or recognized by anyone in Sheffield.

Mrs. Hughes moved close to me and spoke in a low voice, though no one was near. "There is something I must tell you, my dear. Once I introduce you to Andrew Melville, master of Mary's household, I shall be leaving you."

At first I wasn't sure what she meant. My attention was caught by a lad hitching a horse to a cart. My small trunk had already been loaded onto it. The boy's back was toward me, but something about his sure, quick movements seemed familiar.

"Did you hear me?" Mrs. Hughes stepped closer.

"You mean we won't be sleeping in the same room?"

"No, that's not it." Her voice was urgent. "I'll be leaving the castle."

I stared. "But, but I thought . . . I thought you would stay as my chaperone!"

"Then you misunderstood. A young girl requires a chaperone for a journey. But that won't be necessary at Sheffield Castle," she explained. "Your position as a musician is more akin to a servant. Servant girls do not have chaperones."

She was speaking the truth, I realized. I now saw that my trunk was the only luggage on the cart. Mrs. Hughes's bag must now be in this inn, where I supposed she would stay the night before returning to London—or wherever she hailed from.

I swallowed hard. "But . . . Sir Francis said . . . he promised I'd be safe."

"I've known Sir Francis for a long time," she said. "If he makes a promise, he keeps it."

I stared at my feet. I'd gotten rather used to Mrs. Hughes these past few days. At least I felt I could depend on her good sense. But now . . .

"I . . . I'm not sure I can do this alone, Mrs. Hughes," I whispered.

"That's something else I know about Sir Francis Walsingham, Emilia," Mrs. Hughes said, using my real name for the first time. "If he believes you can do something, then you can. And I believe you can too."

"Can't you stay for just a few days?"

"This is no ordinary household, my dear. Master Andrew Melville is in charge of the queen's staff. He won't want to feed me, for one thing. Also, he might suspect I'm a spy from Sir Francis Walsingham and we can't have that." She gave a soft chuckle.

"Just do your best," she went on. "And remember, if

I'm not there, you're more likely to be thrown in with the queen's ladies."

"I don't understand why you're only telling me now," I complained. I felt hungry and sore from all the bouncing and bumping along on muddy roads. I wanted to be home, in the cozy room I shared with Fannie, not heading into a strange castle.

"I didn't tell you before because I didn't want you to stew about it," said Mrs. Hughes. She placed her hand on my arm. "Don't fret. Nothing bad will happen. You are there as a gesture of goodwill from Elizabeth herself."

It seemed to me there couldn't be *that* much goodwill between queens who wished the other one dead. "But what if someone suspects me?"

"I doubt anyone will. There are no obvious ties between you and Sir Francis. And remember this, Emilia: No one notices servants," Mrs. Hughes said. "Also, the Scots queen is fond of dogs, so your big-eyed little friend here might prove helpful."

I opened my mouth to say more, but a cheerful ruddy-cheeked man came across the yard toward us and doffed his hat. "Hello, my goodwomen. My son's got your trunk loaded, but seems like I have to drive you myself. I've been shorthanded these last few days and my lad is needed in the kitchen."

The Plot to Kill a Queen

I wish I could have taken Mouse on long walks through the Sheffield countryside. Instead, like Mary, Queen of Scots, herself, I spent my time in southern Yorkshire cooped up in a horrid damp castle.

"We are grateful for your time, sir," said Mrs. Hughes. "I hope a busy innkeeper like you has a good helpmeet in a wife."

"Aye, I do," he said, with a wide grin. "Though she's been away and, I must admit, I can't do without her."

The dusk was gathering now. And though Mrs. Hughes sat beside me for the two-mile ride to the castle, I felt alone, wrapped in anxiety as thick as my cloak. That feeling only worsened when I got my first glimpse of the castle, looming dark and foreboding on a hill overlooking a spot where two rivers joined.

The innkeeper spoke over his shoulder. "The castle has stood here for three hundred years. Some of the stone walls are as thick as a man is tall. There's only one way in and out, a bridge over the moat. Quite a sight, isn't it?"

"Indeed it is, sir. And this is such a lovely road through the deer park," observed Mrs. Hughes. "Since you run a busy inn, I don't imagine you and your wife get much of a chance to go for drives in the country."

The innkeeper chuckled and winked at her over his shoulder. I turned to stare at her. My insides were quivery with fright, but Mrs. Hughes was flirting with an innkeeper! Was this the same stern, boring widow I'd traveled with for the past three days? I could only suppose her mood was brighter since she was about to be rid of me.

"Ah, here we are, then," said the innkeeper. "Hold your nose."

The cart rumbled over the bridge, and the foul, dank smells of the moat below rose up to sting my nostrils. Mouse shivered in the satchel and whined.

"It's all right, Mousekin," I whispered. "I won't let you fall in."

Act II, Scene 4, Office of Andrew Melville, Master of the Household, Sheffield Castle

"I'm not in favor of this lass being here," grumbled Andrew Melville of Garvock. He glanced at me with hooded eyes and growled, "Just another mouth to feed. If we needed a musician, I could have found someone from Scotland."

I moved a little behind Mrs. Hughes, wishing her skirts were wide enough to hide me. I glanced over at my chaperone, but she was smiling politely, unfazed by his grumbling. I took a breath. Sir Francis and Mrs. Hughes had both warned me not to expect a warm welcome from Mary's Scottish staff. They were right: Master Melville's manner was as chilly as the castle air. He hadn't invited us to sit or even risen from his desk to greet us.

"Well, I suppose she'll have to stay. Her Majesty thinks too highly of her royal cousin in London to say no," Master Melville was saying in a deep, gravelly growl. He pointed a long finger at me. "Are you skilled, lass?"

"I hope to please Her Majesty, sir," I said, dipping a curtsy. "My family has played at the Tudor court for many years."

"The Tudors," said Master Melville, spitting out the word in ill-disguised disgust. "And how is Elizabeth Tudor treating her Stuart cousin? Look at this decaying castle."

Andrew Melville was right about one thing. On the outside, Sheffield was impressive. Inside, I could already feel its soggy dankness seeping into my skin. I wondered if there was a dungeon. Master Melville certainly sounded as if he'd like to put me in one.

"You will be under the charge of Mistress Elizabeth Curle, one of Her Majesty's trusted ladies from Scotland," Master Melville informed me. "Assisting Mistress Curle will be an English girl, Bessie Pierrepont. Are you listening, Mistress Bassano?"

"Yes, sir," I murmured, swaying a little. A wave of exhaustion swept over me. All I wanted was to put my head down and sleep, my little dog nestled next to me.

I wish we'd been able to go inside the Rose and Crown Inn for something to eat—even bread and butter would've been welcome. Instead, Mrs. Hughes had bustled us out of sight behind the inn; I supposed she didn't want anyone gossiping about me.

"I'm just a little worn out from the journey, sir," I told the master of the household now. "May I . . . Would it be all right to inquire where Mousekin and I will sleep?"

"Mousekin? What's a Mousekin?"

"Oh, that's her little pup," Mrs. Hughes said quickly. "Quiet as a mouse it is too, sir. And may I just say you are

The Plot to Kill a Queen

to be congratulated for managing all aspects of a royal household under what clearly are challenging conditions."

Why was stern-faced Mrs. Hughes speaking so sweetly? Then I remembered Fannie's words: "Never underestimate the power of flattery."

Master Melville's mood softened a little. He began bragging about how dogs and birds and, indeed, all creatures under the sun loved Mary. She kept her own aviary and had several pet dogs. He did think it a shame that Elizabeth, who should be more merciful, mostly forbade her cousin from what she loved above all else: riding through the deer park, walking freely in nature, and enjoying good, fresh air.

At last, Mrs. Hughes cleared her throat. "Again, we thank you for your gracious welcome. I'll return for Mistress Bassano in early November. If I am required earlier, a message sent to Daniel Field at the Rose and Crown will reach me. May I presume my young friend here will be given something to eat before she retires?"

Master Melville nodded absently, waving his hand as though such details were beneath him. Which, I thought, they probably were. And which also meant the prospects of getting a meal were low.

I heard a rustle behind me. "Ah, here is Mistress

Pierrepont," said the manager. "She'll show you to your room. Bessie, a word first."

"Thank you, sir." I bowed and followed Mrs. Hughes out.

As we stood alone in the hall, Mrs. Hughes pulled me to one side. I was startled by the intensity of her gaze. Her wide hazel eyes held mine fast. Mrs. Hughes, I suddenly realized, was more vibrant than she'd let on. She had indeed been playing a part.

Now she spoke urgently, her hands firm on my shoulders. "Be a credit to your father, Emilia," Mrs. Hughes whispered. "He was a gentle spirit, a fine, brave man."

My heart slammed hard against my ribs. Mrs. Hughes had known Papa? But how? And, once again, why was she only telling me now?

I opened my mouth to ask, but it was too late. The next instant, my chaperone was swishing quickly down the corridor, a new spring to her step.

"Come on, then," barked Bessie Pierrepont, emerging from Master Melville's office. I slung the strap of my lute over one shoulder, picked up my satchel with Mouse's head poking out, and set out behind her into the dim, dreary innards of the castle.

I truly hoped she wasn't leading me into the dungeon.

The Plot to Kill a Queen

Nine

Act II, Scene 5, The innards of Sheffield Castle

"Keep up! Why are you dawdling?" Bessie Pierrepont demanded, turning around to glare at me.

"I beg your pardon, Mistress Pierrepont. My lute case and satchel are a bit heavy," I replied, forcing myself to speak sweetly. Inwardly I seethed. *Not that you'd offer to help.* And why *did* my satchel seem so heavy? Had Mousekin eaten that much of Horace's gingerbread?

Bessie shot me a haughty look. "I do have other things to do than coddle you. I usually attend Her Majesty in the evenings. Do you even know who I am?"

"Ah . . . um, no. I'm a mere musician and know little of noble society." That, I thought, was mostly true. I was a musician. And if I hadn't sung "Greensleeves" for the queen that day, Her Majesty wouldn't have mentioned my name to Sir Francis. And then he might never have concocted this plan for me to infiltrate Sheffield Castle.

A plan that now seemed like a very bad idea. I couldn't get these people to feed me, let alone reveal their secrets.

But did Bessie have secrets? I wondered. If I was to succeed at this spying enterprise, I should probably start probing that question now. As I pondered how to do that, Bessie was making sure I knew just how superior she was.

"My grandmother is Bess of Hardwick, one of the grandest ladies in the land. She and her current husband, the Earl of Shrewsbury, are entrusted with the care of Mary, Queen of Scots."

"Such an honor..." I murmured. Though I remembered what the gentleman in the coach said: Feeding the royal guest was costing the earl a great deal of money.

"My grandmother sometimes does needlework with the queen. I myself have served Mary since I was little. She is my godmother," Bessie boasted.

Then, with a flounce of her silk gown, she set off again. I hurried to catch up, my mind racing. If Fannie were here, she'd know exactly what to say. She also knew how to read the meaning behind people's words and how to extract secrets. I had to try to do the same. *Be like Fannie*, I told myself.

Deborah Hopkinson

What should I make of what Bessie had just told me? She seemed genuinely fond of the Scots queen. That much was clear. But Bessie was also connected to a prominent English noble family. How far would Bessie's loyalty to Mary go?

If Mary replaced Elizabeth as Queen of England, Bessie wouldn't be tucked away in some old castle. Instead, as one of the ruler's favorites, Bessie would become one of the most powerful young women at court, with rich nobles lining up to seek her hand in marriage.

Of course, no one could suspect the Earl of Shrewsbury or Bess of Hardwick, his wife, of disloyalty to Elizabeth. But Sir Francis had said the Scots queen attracted idealistic young Catholic men, driven by romantic notions of rescuing her. Bessie was ambitious, young, and inexperienced. She'd lived an isolated life here at Sheffield.

What if someone, like one of those well-dressed gentlemen I'd overheard at the Bell Savage Inn, was flattering Bessie, filling her head with foolish dreams? How imprudent was Bessie? Might a young gentleman be able to persuade her to do something risky—as risky as smuggling letters to help her beloved godmother, Mary Queen of Scots? I was mulling these ideas when Bessie spoke again.

"You don't seem very fashionable for someone from London," she said, stopping in the corridor to eye me. "Your cloak is serviceable, I suppose, but your shoes are plain. Though I suppose a musician, even one sent by the queen, is only a servant. And what kind of name is Bassano?"

Goodness, she's annoying! I thought. Still, I couldn't let her make me lose my temper. "It's Italian," I told her sweetly. "My father was from Venice; I get my olive skin from him."

I had to play my part. Here, I wasn't the real Emilia who was constantly questioning and wondering, who had a bold, independent streak, and who wanted to defy custom and become a writer. No, here I had to be an Emilia in awe of Bessie Pierrepont's beauty and style.

Flattery, more flattery. That's what I needed. I tried to imagine what Fannie would say to this snobbish young woman.

"Your fashion sense is exquisite," I told Bessie. "Your gown rivals anything I've seen in London. I am sure you could shine at Elizabeth's court."

"I'm sure I would." Bessie preened. "We may live far from London, but Her Majesty's fashionable wardrobe comes from France. She often gives me pretty gowns. Though I do sometimes wish we had more dances so I could wear them."

I frowned, thinking hard. It was far too soon to cross Bessie off my list entirely. Still, it seemed to me Bessie cared more about clothes than conspiracies. It was hard to envision her as the mastermind of a complicated scheme. That didn't mean she wasn't involved somehow. But I suspected there must be someone else here in the castle who knew more than Bessie. Someone else behind the plot to kill the queen.

And maybe Bessie would let something slip.

I'd have to keep looking. Tomorrow. Right now, I only wanted to collapse into sleep. But Bessie kept leading me upward in this gloomy labyrinth.

At the foot of the next stairwell I had to stop. I took Mouse out and set her on the stone floor. "Stay close now, Mouse. I'm too tired to chase after you."

As I hurried to catch up, my satchel on one shoulder and lute case dangling from the other, I had a sudden memory of bouncing along the corridors of Whitehall Palace on Papa's hip when I was little. I wondered now if Papa had built the lute case to make it easier to carry his instrument and me at the same time.

Bessie flounced onward, her delicate shoes barely making a sound on the cold stone. We turned a corner and headed up another dim stairwell. *Forget the dungeon: They're planning to lock me in the tower,* I thought.

WOOO! Mouse stopped at the foot of the steep stairs. She lifted her small black muzzle into a complaining howl.

"Oh pooh, Mousekin, the stairs aren't that steep!" I cried, exasperated. I trotted back down to sweep her up into the satchel again.

Bessie stopped. "I'm astonished Master Melville has allowed that creature here. Don't expect extra food for her. She must eat off your plate. And you'll be eating with the servants, by the way, not with Mary's valets and ladies.

"Furthermore, your dog had better not bother Geddon, Her Majesty's small, silky terrier," she continued. "If your spaniel so much as touches a hair on his head, you might find her floating in the moat."

I glanced down. Mouse looked up at me with an accusing gaze as if she'd understood every word. I could almost hear her thoughts: "First, you subject me to three days in a bumpy carriage. Now I'm being threatened with the moat! When are we going home to our soft bed and *treats*?"

I swallowed my anger. Flatter. Mollify. Swallow your annoyance. "She'll be no trouble, I promise. Usually she's quiet as a mouse. That's how she got her name. As a puppy she was so tiny and squeaky. Perhaps she and Geddon will play together."

"I doubt that."

Bessie led me up more stone steps, worn from centuries of footsteps. At last she stopped in front of an open door. "That is your chamber. Tomorrow, Mistress Elizabeth Curle will inform you when—or if—you are to play for the queen.

"One more thing. I may not be from London, but I'm

not a foolish country girl. Don't underestimate my power in this household. I'll be watching you."

Then she was gone.

 Act II, Scene 6, A cold turret room in Sheffield Castle

"You're lucky you have fur, Mousekin," I said, stepping into the chilly room.

I looked around. There wasn't much to see. The tiny space was sparsely furnished with a narrow bed with a chamber pot under it, a table by the only window, an oil lamp, a few candles, and a single chair. There was a small hearth in which a weak coal fire had been lit. I didn't think I would be taking off my wool cloak tonight.

My eyes flicked to the corner. My trunk had been carried up, at least. It stood open, my clothes in disarray. It had been searched.

I placed my satchel on the bed and Mouse leaped out. "Why *does* this bag feel so heavy?"

I hadn't opened it on the journey, knowing that my disguise and boots were still nestled on the bottom. And since the bag had been tucked under my feet in the coach, I hadn't noticed its weight. Now I reached down into it. My boys' clothes were wrapped around something hard. What was it?

The Plot to Kill a Queen

I unfolded the fabric and my breath caught. "Oh, look at this, Mouse. It's a writing box!" I cried. "Fannie has given me such a wonderful gift."

I lifted the lid to find reeds for writing, two bottles of ink, paper, and a small purse with some pin money. Something else too: a carefully worded note. I read:

> Dearest Em,
> I know your music will bring joy to all who hear it. Remember, you promised me a good part.
>
> With love, F

"Oh, Mousie, now I can write my play after all," I cried. Maybe it was simply because I was tired, but I had to wipe away tears. Fannie understood.

Fannie understood what I had such a hard time explaining: That I had this deep need, like a hidden spring inside, that kept bubbling up. It was the need to tell a story, and then bring that story to life through the voices of people, of actors. Thanks to Fannie, I would write my play after all.

"Now when I'm not playing, practicing, or sleuthing, I'll write!" I told Mouse as I changed quickly into my nightgown. "It should be easy to imagine Aethelflaed and her family fleeing Viking invaders as we shiver in this old medieval castle."

In fact, I was shivering. So I pulled out the remains of Horace's packet and snuggled up to Mousekin. "Now, before we sleep, I have a surprise, Mousie. I've saved one last bit of gingerbread for our supper. We are so lucky. Even though we are far away, our friends haven't forgotten us."

After we'd eaten every last crumb, I pulled Lady Walsingham's cloak around us and we tumbled into sleep.

Ten

Act II, Scene 7, Turret room, early morning; then more smelly castle innards

Boom! Boom! *WOO!* Mousekin threw her muzzle to the sky and yowled. *WOOOOO!*

"Is that thunder?" I shot up. For a moment I felt lost. The shapes, the cold stone walls, the damp dank smell, everything seemed strange. Where was I?

Slowly, it came back: This was no dream. I was in an old castle, high in a turret like a princess in a fairy tale.

Except I wasn't a princess. I was a spy.

It was only when the noise stopped that I realized I'd been hearing drums. Why drums before dawn? I didn't mind being woken by birdsong or a cock's crow. But drums?

Later I found out the English guards beat drums at five

each morning when they changed shifts outside Mary's bedchamber. It seemed a rather cruel way to force the Scots queen to begin each day: *Wake up! You're a prisoner!* It wasn't pleasant for the rest of us either.

"Shush, Mouse," I begged when it was quiet again. "Let's sleep a little longer."

I buried my head under my cloak. I had indeed kept it on since the blanket was thin and ragged. At home, Fannie and I shared a big four-poster bed with soft sheets and a thick featherbed mattress. This mattress seemed to be filled with lumpy straw.

Mousekin grunted, turned around in a tight circle a few times, and then curled up close beside me again. Not for long, though. I'd no sooner drifted off then she bounded out of bed and trotted to the door. *Scratch! Scratch!* I knew what that meant.

I dressed quickly in my simplest everyday outfit. The sun still hadn't risen, but my room faced east, so I could make out the barest outline of rolling hillsides against the lightening horizon. The gentleman in the coach had said Mary was a great horsewoman. What must it be like to be confined in this place, and not be free to gallop through these glorious frosty meadows?

I turned from the window and took a deep breath. I'd never woken up in a place where I knew no one. But then I looked over, and Mouse was staring up at me, tail wagging. I wasn't entirely alone. "All right, my little Mousie. Let's see if we can find our way down to the kitchen courtyard without getting lost."

The hallway was still—it seemed I was the only person staying on this floor. I hadn't brought a candle and it took a few minutes for my eyes to adjust to the shadowy corridor. At the first stairway, I moved close to the wall and gingerly felt my way down, one step at a time. The rough stone wall was damp and cold against my fingers.

"People have walked these halls for three hundred years," I whispered to Mouse. I couldn't help but wonder if medieval knights or ladies had been murdered in these lonely stairwells.

Once, I heard footsteps, echoing eerily in the distance. I stopped until I heard them fade away. I didn't like the idea of strangers creeping along behind me. As I walked, I began to make a map of the castle in my head. I wondered if there were secret, out-of-the-way rooms where people met to pass Mary's coded correspondence back and forth.

"It's strange here, Mousie, as if the castle is full of ghosts. I don't like it," I whispered. Beside me, her nails made a comforting tap-tap-tapping sound on the cold stone. "Stay close."

We kept heading down, and at last we reached ground level. And then we were out.

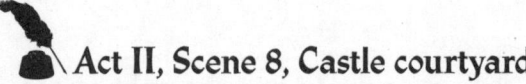 Act II, Scene 8, Castle courtyard

I gulped the cool morning air. It was a relief to step outside, though the castle's high walls felt like a stone monster looming over me.

Mouse took off, nose to the ground, sniffing and snuffling. I stood shivering, still half-asleep, my woolen cloak pulled close around me. The sky had lightened to gray now. Sheffield Castle had been built for defense on a high point—a hill overlooking the confluence of two rivers. Those rivers made the morning mist especially thick and cold and wet.

Yet even so early on a foggy morning, the courtyard was bustling. One wagon piled high with onions, pumpkins, and turnips had pulled up in front of the kitchens to be unloaded. Another cart was rumbling through the enormous gate.

This castle might be isolated, but it was busy. It took a lot of work to feed a captive queen and several dozen of her ladies, valets, chefs, secretaries, and grooms. No wonder the Earl of Shrewsbury was running out of money.

Sheffield's servants were already up and about. I saw a stable boy carrying buckets to a small barn at the far end of the courtyard. A groom was leading a horse around a paddock. A boy was sweeping the courtyard stones in a slow motion, as if he were still half-asleep too.

The boy made me think of Horace, who sometimes complained of having to report to the kitchens before dawn to bake bread for the day. I smiled a little, thinking of how my friend had risen so early to make treats for Mouse and me for our journey. Horace would be up now too, far from here, working in the palace kitchens.

Just a few weeks in this strange place, I told myself. *Then I'll be back in London. And if I work hard, I'll have my play ready to submit to the Master of the Revels.*

I was just wondering whether I should go in search of breakfast when a skinny young maidservant came toward me with a basket of eggs. She turned to wave to one of two lads heading off in the now-empty farmer's wagon. One was hunched low, adjusting his boot. But the driver turned around to wave at the girl. She bounced a little as she called, "Farewell, Nathan!"

When she turned back toward me, the skip in her step sent an egg flying out of her basket. I leaned forward and, lifting my skirts, caught it gently, moving with it to slow its motion.

"Got it!" I cried, holding the unbroken egg aloft with a triumphant flourish.

"Heigh-ho! Now that's a good trick!" cried the girl. She sported a bright, wide smile and startling blue eyes, like robin's eggs. She giggled as I placed the egg back in her basket. "Thank you. You've saved me from Cook's scolding.

"You're the girl lute player from London everyone's talking about, aren't you?" she went on. "They say you've met the queen."

She leaned close and added, "The real one."

I grinned. "Yes, I'm Emilia and this is Mouse. At home, Mouse has a leather ball she likes to chase, so we're lucky she didn't lunge for your egg. Sit, Mouse, and say good morrow nicely."

Mouse sat, wiggling her behind. *Woof!* Mousekin always seemed to sense who was a friend (and who was not).

"I'm Rebecca Alice, though everyone calls me Alice. And hello to you, little waggy tail," said Alice, grinning down at Mouse. "You have such long eyelashes! And a sweet little nose. I'd bend and pet you but I might drop all my eggs. Then I'd truly be in trouble."

I thought of Horace again, and how he suffered under the short tempers of the palace cooks. That much seemed the same here. "Was that a friend in the wagon?" I asked.

"Aye, that's Nathan. His father is the innkeeper in town."

The Plot to Kill a Queen

Oh, that's why he seems so familiar, I thought. I wasn't sure about the other lad, but I'd seen Nathan yesterday, loading my trunk onto the cart. And maybe somewhere else: Could these have been the two lads that helped free our coach from the mud? That hadn't been far from Sheffield.

"Nathan often delivers vegetables, fish, and other supplies here," said Alice as we walked toward the door. "He brings me word of my family sometimes too. Mum let me go into service this summer, once I'd turned twelve. I get awful homesick for our farm still. But as a maid here, I get eight pence a week and my meals as well."

"I wouldn't like living in this castle for long, even in the summer," I said. "I hope you have woolen stockings for the winter. It's only early October but I felt cold last night."

"I'm dreading winter," agreed Alice with a sigh. "Mum has promised to knit me some warm things. I've made up my mind to get through it, though. If I do well here, I hope to get work in one of the earl's other estates, like Sheffield Manor, come spring. The manor is newer and more comfortable. Not like this horrid, smelly old place!"

"It really is awfully cold and damp. It hardly seems fit for a queen, even an imprisoned one," I said. All at once, my stomach growled. "Do the servants eat breakfast near here? I'm ravenous and I expect poor little Mouse is too."

"Aye, there's a room off the kitchens. We can go in together." Alice touched my arm. "You're not taking your meals with Mary's ladies and secretaries?"

I shook my head. "Oh, no. Bessie Pierrepont told me to eat with the servants. I'm glad for it. It'll be easier for me to slip food to Mouse this way. Bessie also said I shouldn't expect extra for her."

"Oh, that Bessie Pierrepont!" Alice rolled her eyes. She leaned close and whispered, "I call her Mistress Pompous Pierrepont.

"And don't worry about your sweet pup," Alice added. "I can squirrel away a plate of leftovers for her every night and sneak it to you. That's how meals work here. The queen and her senior retainers eat first, with all the food arranged on a sideboard. Then everyone else gets the leftovers. The kitchen cats are last. You're in that tiny turret room, aren't you?"

I nodded. "It's . . . it's rather dreary."

"Dreary isn't the half of it. But I should thank you. I was in that room myself. I was only able to move yesterday because they wanted it for you." Alice's blue eyes twinkled as she added, "Though now I'm in with a girl who snores as loud as my old granddad."

We'd reached the door, and Alice stopped. "It's through here. Now, don't mind this lot. I'm afraid they're not very friendly."

Act II, Scene 9, Servants' breakfast table

Alice led me forward into a low-ceilinged room where about two dozen people were already seated around a long wooden table. Everyone turned to stare. I stopped short and dipped a quick curtsy. I felt my face get hot with all those eyes on me. No one smiled.

I scuttled after Alice to the far end of the room, Mouse clicking along behind me. Alice pointed. "You can sit here. I'll join you once I've put my basket down," Alice whispered. "The bread's there along with beer, ale, cider, and apples. Have as many apples as you like. The castle has its own trees and we get some from local orchards too."

I took a cup of cider, an apple, and two slices of bread. Then, checking to be sure no one was watching, I snared another piece of bread for Mouse. I slipped into an empty seat. Luckily, the chatter at the table had started up again and I didn't feel quite so conspicuous.

- ASIDE -

You may well wonder why so many people in my time drink ale or beer for breakfast—and indeed throughout the day. The reason, of course, is simple. Water carries diseases and makes us sick.

Most adults in my time drink about a gallon of beer daily. Beer is made from water, malt barley, and hops. Beer will keep longer than ale. Ale, made from barley, doesn't have hops and should be drunk within three days.

As I munched my apple, I remembered Sir Francis's advice: Watch and listen. I soon realized that the servants at the far end of the table mostly spoke Scots, a language I didn't understand. They were members of Mary's own household who'd left Scotland to serve her. Mrs. Hughes had told me that although Mary was imprisoned, she was allowed to live like a queen with her own domestic staff, including servants, ladies-in-waiting, valets, secretaries, and chefs.

The English servants clustered at my end of the table. "No one in that unhappy place will welcome you," Mrs. Hughes had warned on our last evening as we ate a hot dinner in a private room at an inn. "The earl's servants resent being assigned to a prisoner in his least comfortable estate. And the Scottish folks resent the fact that their beloved Mary has been kept a prisoner for so many years."

"If no one talks to me, won't it be hard to find out anything?" I asked.

"Unhappy people love to complain," Mrs. Hughes told me. "Listen closely. Find out who is in the queen's innermost circle. Remember, the person helping Mary smuggle letters has her complete trust. Look for that person."

"Will it be a Scottish servant for certain?" I asked.

"Not necessarily. Mary spent part of her girlhood in France and may have a trusted French secretary or servant. But remember, anyone can be bought," she went on. "That's another reason Sir Francis is sending you now. He's worried that agents he once trusted may have been bribed to work for Mary and against Elizabeth."

Anyone can be bought. I glanced around the table. Was one of these servants key to the mystery of the smuggled letters?

As I ate, I got a strange feeling, as if I was being watched. I glanced up and met the eyes of an English guard across the table. I looked away quickly, but not before noticing that he had a square-shaped face and a large, round nose with a bump on it, as if it had been broken.

I could feel his cold gray eyes boring into me, almost as

if he could read my thoughts. Almost as if he knew all my secrets and exactly why I was there.

The bread tasted dry in my mouth. I ate quickly and rose from the table. As I left the room, I could feel the guard's eyes following me every step of the way.

Eleven

Act II, Scene 10, Castle courtyards

"Mouse, come!" I called loudly. "Stop barking at that horse. Now!"

Mousekin gave one last *WOOF!* She trotted over slowly and plunked herself down before me, grinning and wagging her tail, clearly very proud of herself for intimidating the giant creature.

"I love you dearly, Mouse, but by now you should know better than to tease cart horses," I scolded. "Why, that mare's hooves are as big as your head! Let's move to the side where it's safer."

We'd gone out to the courtyard again after breakfast. I didn't expect Mistress Curle to send for me to perform so early in the day—if she sent for me at all. So I took this chance. While Mouse sniffed, I would explore.

I knew secret letters had to be getting to Queen Mary somehow. Also, since there was only one way in and out of the castle, all the wagons and carts making deliveries passed under the grand stone archway. The exchange of letters could be taking place right here. But though I watched awhile, I didn't notice anything suspicious.

Mouse and I meandered over to the large kitchen herb garden, which still boasted a few greens. Nearby, I spotted a small stand of apple and cherry trees. "Look, Mouse. Maybe we can pick some apples off the ground if we get really hungry.

"Mousekin?"

Where *was* she? I spotted Mouse's curly brown tail disappearing behind a hedge. I chased after her and found myself at an ornate iron gate, which stood open. I went through.

"Mouse," I hissed. "Here, Mousie!" Maybe she'd gone after a cat. She always pretended not to hear me when she had something better to do.

I followed the path and soon found myself in a garden—a private walled garden that curved to the left around the side of the castle.

There were no carts here, just shaded walkways

winding through trees and flower beds. On one side stood a small aviary, with cooing turtledoves and plump pigeons. I gulped. That was a clue to where I was: Andrew Melville had mentioned that Mary kept birds.

My hunch was right. To my horror, I saw Mousekin trot over to a group of elegantly gowned ladies. In the center stood a tall, imposing woman holding a small, long-haired, gray-and-silver terrier.

Mouse planted herself and barked, as if to say, "Good morrow. Can your dog play?"

I wanted to shout, "Bow, Mouse!" Because clearly my dog was barking at Mary, Queen of Scots.

I ran forward. What if Mary's guards unleashed their swords on Mousekin? A burly guard leaped out of nowhere in front of me, demanding, "Halt! How did you get in here?"

"The gate was ajar. Please, sir, I mean no harm," I cried. "I'm a guest. I only want to fetch my dog."

Frantically, I looked around. "You can ask Bessie Pierrepont there. She knows who I am." I waved and Bessie nodded to the guard, who ran off to check the gate, grumbling about one of his new men being careless.

Meanwhile, Mary bent down and let loose her little terrier, who hurtled around in circles. He yapped in delight, Mousekin at his heels. This must be Geddon. The dogs

The Scots queen and I had something in common: a love of dogs. Her little terrier, Geddon, was her favorite.

streaked and tumbled like puppies, wrestling and barking. Then they flopped in a heap at Mary's feet, where they chewed on each other's ears, squealing if the play bites were too hard.

I took a few steps forward, unsure whether to approach. Then the Scots queen scooped up Mousekin and came toward me. I bowed low, something I'd practiced with Lady Walsingham before accompanying Fannie to court.

"Should you meet the queen, keep your eyes lowered and only speak if she speaks to you first," Lady Walsingham had instructed. She'd been talking about Elizabeth. But I did the same now.

"Does anyone know this young person, whom I presume is the owner of this energetic creature who has captured Geddon's heart?" the Scots queen called over her shoulder. "Do you, Mistress Curle?"

One of the fashionable ladies stepped forward to address the queen. So this was Mistress Elizabeth Curle, who would determine when I performed for the queen. "The girl plays the lute, Your Majesty; she was sent by your cousin in London to entertain you for a few weeks."

Bessie Pierrepont piped up, "Her name is Emilia Bassano, Your Majesty."

"You may rise, Mistress Bassano. Tell me, why has my cousin sent you here, child?" the Scots queen said. She spoke with a soft French accent. Her cloak was velvet and she wore a gold ring with a sparkling ruby. Necklaces of pearl and amber adorned her neck. Her skin looked soft and clear, and I wondered if it was true that she bathed in white wine.

"Your Majesty, I am part of the Bassano family." I curtsied once more, keeping my eyes lowered. "My father and his brothers came from Italy years ago to perform for King Henry. Queen Elizabeth hopes my music will please you."

"King Henry was my great-uncle, my grandmother's brother," she said. The queen held out Mousekin. "Now tell me, do you also play for my sister queen, who keeps me here in dreadful confinement?"

I took Mouse, and kept my eyes cast down. "My cousins are court musicians; I do sometimes join them."

I peeked up from under my lashes. Bessie Pierrepont was staring at me, an annoyed look on her face. Perhaps she didn't like the queen's attention on anyone but herself.

"You are welcome here, Mistress Bassano. I do not mind a guest who brings this sweet creature. I love dogs, songbirds, and horses, though I am less fond of cats." Mary's smile seemed sad. "We shall look forward to hearing your lute."

I bowed once more. Then, to my astonishment, the queen stepped closer.

"Child, do you, perhaps, carry a special message for me from my sister queen, Elizabeth?" she asked in a low voice. "Is she, at last, willing to show her poor cousin mercy? I would gladly return to France. Or even better, rule beside my son in Scotland. I miss my child so much. He is just a little older than you now. I am not even allowed to write to him and fear his advisors have turned him against me."

The Plot to Kill a Queen

I thought, suddenly, of the empty birdcage I'd seen in the attic of the Bell Savage Inn. I didn't see how Mary could survive this stone cage of a castle. But did she merely want her liberty, or was she desperate enough to plot to kill Elizabeth?

"I . . . I have no special message, Your Majesty, except my own presence as a gesture of goodwill," I stammered. "People say the gentle strains of the lute bring comfort and peace, and I hope my songs will do that."

I glanced up. Her eyes were fixed on me, searching my face. What did she hope to find? Was she trying to discern whether I was lying?

For it was a lie. I wasn't there to give comfort. I was there to find out the truth about her treacherous plotting.

Do not feel sorry for Mary, she is dangerous, I reminded myself. *She would have Elizabeth killed and take her throne. She plots with other countries against England.*

Mary sighed. "Very well, child, we will send for you to play when the time is convenient."

I bowed low, then backed away.

As I approached the gate, I saw that a guard was now posted there. I wondered if any of these guards might be secret Catholics aligned with Mary's cause? The gate was hidden by shrubbery. Maybe a guard could be bribed to leave it unlocked, as it was this morning, to let someone in—or out.

There might even be a hiding place nearby for letters, I thought. But though I scanned the ground, I saw no large stones or crevices. Besides, the gateway to the queen's courtyard seemed too obvious.

"Foolproof," I'd heard the man say about the new method of smuggling letters. No, I'd have to keep looking.

I was almost to the gate when I heard quick footsteps behind me. I whirled and found myself face-to-face with Elizabeth Curle. She grabbed my arm. "You are a sly little fox, letting your dog loose to worm your way into Her Majesty's heart."

"I . . . I assure you, Mistress Curle," I stammered. "I didn't mean . . ."

She cut me off. Her whole face, her entire being, seemed contorted in anger. "My good lady may be inclined to trust you. I do not. Nor do we trust her Tudor cousin, that imposter on the throne. Watch your step here."

Mistress Curle stormed off, her silk gown rustling. I stood frozen, my breathing ragged. Bessie Pierrepont might be too frivolous to be seriously engaged in plotting. Yet it was clear Elizabeth Curle would do anything for the Scots queen. Anything.

The Plot to Kill a Queen

- SOLILOQUY -

Like an aside, but longer, a **soliloquy** is a speech where someone turns to the audience to share thoughts. The most famous soliloquy is from Shakespeare's *Hamlet*.

I was at Sheffield Castle to spy, but I had another task as well: to write a play about the ancient warrior queen Aethelflaed.

Aethelflaed must have been unusually gifted to be a female leader in medieval times. Queen Elizabeth is brave too. She has refused to marry, defying the advice of her counselors, and indeed all tradition. I think she has done so because to marry would mean giving up her power and authority to a husband.

And it seems to me that Mary, Queen of Scots, has a kind of courage too. Imprisoned in this castle, she still fights for her freedom.

I wonder if women leaders of the future will face the same challenges. Will society still believe that, even with a woman as queen, the rest of us aren't equal to men?

My play is about Aethelflaed, who lived seven hundred years ago. What will the world be like seven hundred years from now, or even five hundred? Why, five hundred years would be 2082. It seems so far away.

I can only hope that by then things will have changed. I hope that anyone who wants to can go to college, write books, act onstage, enter a profession, help to make laws, and lead nations. It does seem change takes far too much time. But surely five hundred years is enough!

Twelve

Act II, Scene 11, Turret room

"Mistress Curle is rather terrifying, don't you think?" I whispered to Mouse as we climbed back up to our cold chamber. "Though I can't help feeling a little sorry for Mary, especially when she spoke of her son. Imagine being a prisoner in this smelly old place for years and years, cut off from the world and your destiny as a queen."

As for Elizabeth Curle, I didn't think flattery was likely to work with this lady—it would be like trying to flatter a deadly snake.

"At least you made friends with Geddon," I said, sitting down at the table and setting out my writing materials. "And since we're likely to be stuck in this little room, I shall begin to write my play. I might even get the first scene done. Because after my encounter with Mistress Curle, I doubt I'll be summoned to entertain Mary today."

In that, however, I was wrong.

∞

Rap!

Woof! Woof!

I startled awake as Mouse set up a frantic alarm. I'd tried to write, but felt so sleepy my eyes kept closing. Finally, I'd rested my head on my arm and drifted off, still seated at the table before an empty page. So much for scene one!

So far, I didn't seem to be doing well at either pursuit: spying or playwriting.

Rap! Rap! Rap! "Mistress Bassano? Emilia? Are you there? Open up, it's me!"

I shook myself awake and ran to the door. Mouse joined me, barking, and ready to confront any intruder. "Don't worry, Mouse. It's our friend Alice."

Alice burst in like a fresh breeze and took my hand. "When you didn't come to dinner at midday I began to worry."

"I fell asleep," I admitted. "I'm still tired from the journey."

"You'd better wake up now. I have a message: Mistress

The Plot to Kill a Queen

Curle and Bessie Pierrepont have summoned you to the queen's presence chamber within the hour. Her Majesty would like you to play this afternoon. But first, I've brought you a meat pie. We get leftovers from the queen's meals. There are thirty-two different dishes served at dinner and the same number at supper!"

Alice giggled. "I never imagined I'd taste delicacies like French pastries."

"Oh, thank you. My stomach's grumbling," I said. "And there's enough for Mouse."

"You don't have to share." Alice's eyes sparkled as she knelt before Mouse. "For you, little one, I have bread and a slice of mutton. Enjoy your treat, sweet pup, because you are also commanded to appear. It seems you made quite an impression on Geddon this morning and the royal terrier requests your presence."

"Mouse did indeed charm the Scots queen," I told Alice between mouthfuls. "I didn't do quite as well. We wandered into the queen's private garden and Mistress Curle stormed at me. I'm surprised she asked for me at all."

"The queen must have overruled her, which is unusual; from what I hear, Elizabeth Curle has more influence on the queen than any other lady," Alice said, straightening. "It's said she's the one who cares for all the queen's jewels, including ruby rings and strings of pearls."

"The queen must trust her... a lot," I said aloud. Inwardly I wondered: If Mary did indeed trust Mistress Curle with her most precious treasure, might the queen also rely on her in other matters as well? Was Mistress Curle the key to finding how Mary was sending and receiving secret letters?

"Aye, I've heard Bessie say Elizabeth Curle would lay down her life for Mary," Alice said as I finished my meal. "Now, I don't imagine you have jewels. But do you have something fitting to wear for your appearance in Mary's presence chamber, Emilia?"

"Yes! And if you can spare me a few more minutes, I'd love some help to get ready." My hands flew to my head. "Oh, and my hair!"

"Fear not. Today I shall be your lady's maid, Mistress Bassano." Alice giggled and dipped a curtsy. "I overheard another servant ask Bessie if she should help you dress. Bessie told her no and ordered her to deliver the message to you and leave."

"So you offered to come instead to help me? Oh, thank you, Alice. I expect Bessie and Mistress Curle would relish seeing me disgrace myself by appearing disheveled before the queen."

I finished the pie, then knelt before my trunk. Earlier,

I'd donned a smock of cambric. Now I pulled out items for Alice to place on the bed.

"Bessie means to embarrass me, but I do have some pretty things, mostly borrowed from my friend Fannie, who's a junior lady-in-waiting at court. I'll change these woolen stockings for knitted silk ones, and my simple waistcoat for a fine embroidered one."

I added a corse, a sort of corset. Alice helped me lace it in back, and over that she settled a farthingale. Next, I donned a red petticoat, then Fannie's russet gown with long sleeves.

"I like this ruff; it's not too large," Alice said as she adjusted the white pleated collar around my neck. "It would be hard to do my work with all these layers of clothes."

I almost told Alice about walking around London so freely in my boy's disguise. *Better not*, I reminded myself. I trusted Alice, but Sir Francis had said it would be safer for me to say as little about my real life in London as possible.

Alice smoothed the fabric of my gown and nodded her approval. "You look as fine as any of Mary's ladies. Now I'll work magic on your hair and coif. My older sister is a lady's maid, and whenever we're home at the same time she teaches me."

I took a deep breath. "I'm so grateful, Alice. Thanks to you and Fannie I won't feel too out of place."

"Were you writing a letter to your friend?" Alice asked, gesturing to my writing things on the table.

"A letter? Oh, no..." I hesitated for a moment. Yet I didn't see why I couldn't share this. "I'm writing a story actually, in the form of a play. It's about Princess Aethelflaed, the daughter of King Alfred of Wessex from medieval times."

"I love stories! And I know about King Alfred, who helped unify England," Alice said. "My grandpa always told that old tale of King Alfred and the cakes."

I grinned. "Yes, that's exactly what my play will be about. Only I shall write it with young Princess Aethelflaed as the heroine."

"Will the title be *King Alfred's Daughter*?"

I thought for a minute. "No, I think I'll call it *The Princess Saves the Cakes* since she's the hero. In my story, Aethelflaed arrives at the cottage in time to keep the cakes from burning. She also tries not to disturb her slumbering father, who's weary from leading his people to safety through the night."

"What happens then?"

"That's a good question," I replied, frowning. Alice's questions were helping me realize my play, like all stories, would need a beginning, a middle, and an end.

"I'm not exactly sure what should happen next in the

plot, but I think perhaps the peasant woman predicts Aethelflaed will be a great leader and warrior queen," I told Alice.

"A warrior queen—ooh, that's exciting!" breathed Alice, as she made the last adjustments to my curls. "I especially like the part where she tries to let her father rest. I miss my papa. He should be bringing a load of pumpkins from our fields here this week; I watch for him every day."

"I hope you see him again soon, Alice."

I glanced at my lute; it was my link to Papa. I wondered if Mary had anything she could touch that connected her to her son, James. Mrs. Hughes had told me the Scots queen hadn't seen James since he was less than a year old. Now he was sixteen and she might never see him again.

"Now, twirl," Alice said, clapping her hands. "Oh, Mouse, doesn't your mistress look like a princess herself?"

Mouse woofed and wagged her tail. Alice looked over at the table and frowned. "Before we go, I don't think you should leave your writing materials out—or anything you don't want anyone to see."

"I thought someone went through my trunk last night!" I cried. "Do you think Andrew Melville or Elizabeth Curle will have my room searched again?"

"It's possible." Alice nodded. "They don't trust anyone from London. That's why the queen's chefs are French:

Mary fears being poisoned. But I have an idea to keep your writing things safe. When I lived in this room I discovered a secret hiding place."

Alice crawled under the table and wriggled a stone out from the wall. "I found this loose stone one day as I was cleaning. When I pried it open, I discovered a large empty crevice in the wall."

"Does anyone else know about it?" I packed up my writing box and handed it down to her.

Alice shook her head. "Only me."

I peeked under the table as she placed the box in the crevice. "Is there more room in the crevice?"

"Yes, it's larger than it seems. Do you have something else to hide?"

"No, just curious," I replied. I wondered if I should stash my disguise in there too. For now, though, it could stay in the bottom of the satchel under Mouse's blanket.

It was time to go, so I placed Mouse in the satchel. "I'd better keep her in it when we're in the queen's presence chamber. Bessie threatened to throw Mouse in the moat if she causes trouble."

Alice rolled her eyes. "I wondered if you would be like Bessie, you being from London and all. I'm very glad you're not."

The Plot to Kill a Queen

I laughed. "Alice, I don't think anyone in London is as pompous as Bessie Pierrepont."

Act II, Scene 12, The innards of Sheffield Castle

I closed my door, slinging my lute strap over my shoulder. Alice picked up the satchel. "I can carry this for you, at least part of the way. I'll show you where to go, but then I've got to hurry back to the kitchen. I'll come back tonight with more food and some scraps for Mouse and you can tell me all about it."

"Have you ever been in the queen's presence chamber?" I whispered as our footsteps echoed in the dark stone corridors.

"No, the queen's Scottish housemaids tend the fires there." Alice turned a corner and beckoned me forward. "This way is shorter."

I followed, wondering if I'd ever learn my way around. "The queen seems to have a large staff."

"They say when she first arrived in England, Mary had money to pay them, but that's run out," Alice whispered. "At one point she had sixty; now I think it's about thirty people.

"The gossip downstairs is that the earl would like to

be stricter with Mary and make her cut costs," she went on. "But he's afraid to be too stingy or mean. If something should happen to Elizabeth, there's still a chance Mary would become Queen of England."

"If something happened?" I asked. "What do you mean?"

"Anything." Alice shrugged. "Perhaps a fever or the plague."

"What about other possibilities? Like assassination plots," I whispered. "Do you hear talk of them here?"

Alice turned to me, eyes wide. "Plots? You're not . . . a secret Catholic who's against Elizabeth?"

"No! I only meant that, sometimes in London one hears about plots against Elizabeth. And some say those plots start here."

"I know nothing," Alice murmured. "It's best not to talk about this. Someone might get the wrong idea."

"I won't mention it again," I assured her. And I wouldn't. I hadn't really expected Alice to know anything about smuggled letters. After all, she hadn't been at Sheffield long and was one of the youngest servants here. I didn't want her to think I was anything other than a lute player. And I definitely didn't want to cause her trouble for befriending me.

We'd reached a long corridor and Alice stopped. "Walk down this hallway. About halfway, you'll see a guard, or maybe two, posted outside the presence chamber. Just give your name and say that Mistress Curle sent for you."

Alice grinned, her blue eyes bright with mischief. "Be prepared to be surprised. It's not at all like your turret room."

She hurried off with light footsteps, while I made my way along the corridor. I gave my name to the guard and he opened the great wooden doors.

Act II, Scene 13, Presence chamber of Mary, Queen of Scots

I took a few steps into the grand hall and almost gasped aloud. Mouse popped up her head; even she seemed in awe. Alice was right: This was nothing like my spare, frosty room in the turret or the smelly, damp stone corridors of the castle.

Here, bright Turkish carpets covered the floors; rich tapestries adorned the walls. Several chairs on a dais at the front of the room sported coverings that shimmered in gold and red. These chairs seemed to be reserved for the queen and her special guests, while her ladies sat on low stools clustered near a window, where the light was better for needlework. A side table boasted silver bowls filled with apples and a silver platter piled high with pastries.

Mary had become a queen when she was only six days old. She was a prisoner, yet she demanded her due: to be treated like royalty. This room was nothing more than a gilded cage.

But Mary still believed herself a queen. And at that moment I felt it was true.

Thirteen

Act II, Scene 13 continued, Presence chamber of Mary, Queen of Scots

Why send for me if she doesn't want me to play? I thought crossly. I'd been sitting on this stool at the back of the great hall for at least an hour. I blew softly on my fingers to warm them. It would be hard to pluck my lute strings with stiff, chilled fingers. My muscles ached from the cold.

"Wait here," Bessie had ordered. She'd come to where I stood, mouth open, and looked me up and down, surprise on her face. I had to keep from smiling. Thanks to Fannie and Alice, Bessie could find nothing in my appearance to criticize.

"If Her Majesty wants you to perform, one of her ladies

will give you a signal. Strum sweetly. No sad or melancholy songs, just pleasant music," Bessie instructed.

She'd glanced at the leather satchel by my side. Mouse peeked out, her small chin resting on the edge. Mousie opened one eye a little, but closed it again. Although my spaniel was the perfect slumbering guest, Bessie hissed, "Do not let that creature bark."

"Yes, Mistress Pierrepont," I replied quietly, dipping a curtsy. Inwardly I seethed: *Pooh, she is bossy!*

I took my place on the stool she indicated and looked around curiously, taking in the splendor of the lavishly decorated hall. Bessie returned to the other ladies. I tried to listen, but was too far away to hear any conversation. I shifted in frustration. If I was kept far back in this cold corner, I'd never learn anything that might shed light on the smuggled letters.

I could still watch closely, though. Right away, I noticed Bessie was seated a little behind a small semicircle of older ladies. It made me wonder. The Scots queen, missing her own child, might dote on Bessie and buy her pretty things. But Bessie was only fifteen: Would Mary trust her with serious confidential matters?

Next I looked at the other ladies. Elizabeth Curle was there, of course, with four other women. These, I guessed,

The Plot to Kill a Queen

were "the four Marys." Mrs. Hughes had told me these ladies (all named Mary!) had been the Scottish queen's companions since she was a girl.

Before she turned six, Mary had been betrothed to a French prince. For her safety, because of trouble between England and Scotland, the young queen had been sent to live in France. Francis, her future bridegroom, was only four. Eventually Mary did marry her French prince, but he died at sixteen after just a year as king. (Poor Mary! No wonder Elizabeth had decided not to marry.)

Since these ladies-in-waiting had been with the queen for almost her entire life, I thought any one of the "four Marys" could be at the heart of the plot to help her escape and reign again. But I wasn't even sure I could learn to tell them apart.

And that brought me back, once again, to Elizabeth Curle.

My eyes narrowed as I focused on her. She sat closer to the queen's raised dais than anyone else. I saw that whenever Mary wanted something to drink or needed more colored threads for her embroidery, she called on Mistress Curle first. Alice was right: Mary definitely trusted Elizabeth Curle.

I needed to keep watching Mistress Curle, not only here but elsewhere in the castle too. Though I had a feeling that, just like a snake, this lady could slither unseen in the shadows—and then strike when least expected.

※

At last, when I felt I might turn into an icicle, Mistress Curle beckoned me forward. I moved to a stool close to the queen's ladies, who sat clustered like petals of a flower.

I chose pleasant, soothing tunes, and some of Queen Elizabeth's favorites, including "Scarborough Fair," an old ballad Papa had taught me. He'd gotten interested in folk songs as a boy in Italy and had enjoyed learning English music too.

"In centuries past, songs moved as people traveled and traded," he told me. "Consider 'Scarborough Fair.' It's set in the north of Yorkshire, England, but the lyrics echo a Scottish song called 'The Elfin Knight.'"

After I'd played for a little while, the queen called out, "Geddon is waking up from his nap. Did you bring your spaniel?"

I rose and curtsied deeply. "Yes, Your Majesty. Mouse is here."

"Let them frolic," she commanded. "And while they do, you can sing for me. You do sing, I presume?"

"A little, Your Majesty."

The Plot to Kill a Queen

"Come closer." She pointed. "Stand there and sing 'The Elfin Knight.'"

"I beg your pardon, Your Majesty. I only know the lyrics to the English version, 'Scarborough Fair.'"

"Very well, then."

And so, as the two dogs wrestled on the bright carpet at my feet, I began:

> *"O, where are you going?"*
> *"To Scarborough fair,"*
> *Savory, sage, rosemary, and thyme;*
> *"Remember me to a lass who lives there,*
> *For once she was a true love of mine."*

"That was lovely, my child. Tomorrow, come again and sing 'Greensleeves' for me," the queen commanded. "That tune makes me think of my own child far away."

She sighed and added, almost to herself, "Already sixteen—what a fine lad he must be!"

I curtsied and returned to the back of the hall, Mouse trotting reluctantly at my heels. I bent down to pack up my lute and place Mousekin in my satchel again. As I straightened, a messenger—at least I presumed he was a messenger—arrived.

This fashionable gentleman had a long, distinctive mustache. Dressed impeccably in a rich velvet doublet, he sported a large, ostentatious ruff. I smiled a little, thinking how Horace liked to make fun of men who donned such fripperies. "When these fellows get caught in a rain shower, their starched and pleated ruffs flop and droop so it looks like they're wearing the dishcloths I use in the palace kitchens."

Rushing forward, the gentleman bumped against the lute case that dangled from my left shoulder. He stopped and bowed. "Pardonnez-moi, mademoiselle. I do beg your pardon. I am ever the clumsy oaf. I should most assuredly have noticed a lovely young lady such as you."

He bowed again and shot me a dazzling smile; I dipped a curtsy and even smiled back. It was hard not to. *A charming gentleman*, I thought, *though he's rather a flirt*.

He looked quite modern too—like a young gentleman I'd see every day on a London street or in the elegant extravagance of Elizabeth's court. Yet he seemed out of place here in this clammy, dark medieval castle far from the big city. When I walked these stone corridors, I imagined fierce knights of old carrying lances, their armor clanking—not gentlemen wearing velvet doublets and pleated white ruffs.

I did, however, notice that the newcomer had a note in his hand. Would he bring it to Mary himself? To delay,

The Plot to Kill a Queen

I bent down to settle Mouse more securely. Meanwhile, I watched under my lashes as the man made his way to the front of the hall. He stopped for a moment beside Bessie, and leaned over to whisper something to her. Even from here, I could see her smile and blush.

He seems charming, but perhaps a silly sort of man, I thought. But then he lingered a moment and I wondered: Is this simply a flirtation or do Bessie and the gentleman truly like each other? If Bessie dressed to please this stylish gentleman, that might help explain her own love of fashion.

I kept watching and my eyes widened. Elizabeth Curle had risen from her seat and stood squarely before the queen's dais. She held out her hand and took the note. "Merci, Monsieur Nau. I will take this."

At that moment, Mistress Curle glanced across the hall at me, her gaze stern. I wished I could linger to see what would happen next. But even from a distance, she made it clear she wanted me to leave.

✿

That day was the beginning. After that, the queen sent for Mousekin and me every afternoon and evening. I was performing so much I had to find new tunes to play. I'd perfected the pieces I'd brought with me. I'd even gotten up the courage to ask Mistress Curle to borrow a partbook, a volume of printed music with notes for instrument and voice that I'd seen on a side table.

Without Alice's help, I'd never have managed. Mid-morning, when Alice had a break from her kitchen duties, she helped me change into one of my gowns. She returned in the evening to unlace me. Alice also brought a late supper, enough for me (and, of course, Mouse), since by the time the servants ate the queen's leftovers, I was back performing in Mary's presence chamber.

"Alice, thank you for feeding us—and for everything," I said one evening. "You have a gift for fashion. Neither Bessie nor Mistress Curle has found fault with my appearance."

"I suppose it's ambitious for a farm girl, but I'd like to be a lady's maid or a seamstress for a noble family someday," Alice said. "I love working with beautiful fabrics."

Mouse was doing her part too. My spaniel and Geddon chased each other round and round, then curled up together on the rug. The queen would laugh at their antics while embroidering or sketching new panels she planned to create. Needlework seemed to be one of the few enjoyments left to her.

But though I spent time in the queen's presence chamber each day, I was no closer to finding any answers. How would I face Sir Francis and tell him I had failed? And what if my failure meant danger—or even death—for Queen Elizabeth?

Fourteen

🖋 **Act II, Scene 14, Turret room, a fortnight later**

"We're stuck, Mousekin," I said one morning two weeks later. It was a gray, blustery mid-October day, with dense low clouds that streamed across the skies like a great herd of deer bounding over the landscape.

I threw down my reed and buried my head in my hands. "Mistress Curle may be the person behind Mary's secret correspondence, but without evidence we can't prove a thing. And I can't find a shred of evidence of how letters are getting in—or out."

Just then Alice knocked. "The queen is feeling poorly, and Bessie told me to bring you word not to appear."

"That's all right. Mousekin and I can spend the day

here. She'll curl up and nap. Geddon does tire her out," I said. "And I'll work on Aethelflaed's story."

Alice stepped inside. She patted Mouse and asked, "Have you finished the first scene yet, Emilia?"

"Aye, I have! Aethelflaed has spotted the Viking invaders approaching. Now King Alfred and his followers are trudging through the night to hide in the marshlands of Somerset," I told her.

"I'm eager to hear you read it aloud."

"Just knowing you want me to keep going helps a lot and I hope I finish it before I leave," I said, giving her a quick hug.

And it did help to know at least one person cared. I could imagine Alice listening, her bright blue eyes sparkling with excitement. I thought back to the day Will Shakespeare told me he enjoyed watching the audience fall into the story. An audience.

A play needs an audience, I thought, *just as books need readers.*

An **audience** is the people who watch a performance.

The Plot to Kill a Queen

After Alice left, I sat at the small table, pages spread before me. Sometimes it helped to close my eyes before writing a scene. But my thoughts kept coming back to Elizabeth Curle. I turned over everything I knew. She held a special place in Mary's retinue. She was trusted with the jewels. She was the one who took notes being delivered to the queen in the presence chamber.

She simply *had* to be the key.

Yet I was no closer to discovering how letters were being smuggled into and out of Sheffield Castle and what Elizabeth Curle's precise role in that might be. I was sure the English guards must check regular correspondence and notes such as the one Monsieur Nau had delivered that first day.

That meant there had to be another way: a "foolproof" method the men at the inn playhouse had mentioned.

I sighed and tried to focus on my story again. I didn't have Alice as an audience right now. But I did have Mouse. "King Alfred has just spotted the swineherd's hut. Next he'll knock and ask for shelter," I told my little dog, who'd curled up on the bed in the folds of my woolen cloak.

"I'll finish this scene," I said. "Then later, when Mary and her ladies are at supper, we'll do some sleuthing. There has to be some deserted chamber Mistress Curle uses to exchange secret correspondence. Or maybe there's a room in the cellar with a hidden box where someone from the outside drops letters for Elizabeth Curle to pick up."

I'd already tried to explore the castle corridors. Wandering in these dank, dark spaces made me nervous. Mousekin's toes made a clicking sound on the stone floors, so we weren't exactly silent. Once, just a few days ago, the guard with the broken nose had come around a corner unexpectedly and stood, blocking my way.

"Oh, um, hello, sir," I'd sputtered, dipping a curtsy. "Mouse . . . that is, my little dog here wandered off and I had to go after her. I'm . . . I'm just trying to reach the courtyard."

He'd grunted and pointed. "That way."

Since then, I'd avoided that guard whenever I could. Rather than face his stony glare at breakfast, I simply snatched some bread and apples to bring to my room. I hadn't wandered again in the gloomy stone halls of the castle. But I couldn't put it off any longer.

I shook off the memory of the guard. I'd only written a few more words when I heard footsteps. Someone rapped sharply at the door. I froze.

This was not Alice's knock.

"Mistress Bassano? I need to speak with you." There

was no mistaking that stern commanding tone: Elizabeth Curle.

My writing! My stomach clenched. I couldn't let her see it.

My story about the princess and the cakes was innocent enough. But my role here was that of an uneducated lute player—not a girl who'd studied alongside Fannie Walsingham with some of the best tutors in the land.

Emilia the musician wouldn't be writing a play. And if Mistress Curle found out, she'd be even more suspicious of me.

I had to think fast.

"Good afternoon, Mistress Curle." I opened the door wide so she could peer in, as I knew she wished to do. I curtsied respectfully. "How may I help you?"

Mistress Curle was tall, much taller than me. But I straightened up and lifted my chin. *I won't let her intimidate me*, I thought, trying to keep my breath steady.

Her expression was scornful as her dark eyes grazed my simple outfit. "I see you received the message not to appear in the presence chamber today," she said. "I came to inform you that Her Majesty is recovering and will expect you tomorrow after the midday dinner."

And why have you come yourself instead of sending Bessie or

Alice with that message? I wanted to ask. Aloud I replied, "It will be my pleasure, as always."

She frowned and looked over my head. "What have you been doing?"

I followed her gaze. Mousekin still dozed comfortably atop the cozy-looking nest of my brown cloak. In truth, though, the cloak was rather lumpier than before, since I'd quickly hidden my writing box, with all my supplies stuffed inside, right under it.

Fortunately, I'd also been practicing my lute earlier, and it lay on the bed with the partbook I'd borrowed, partially blocking Mistress Curle's view of Mouse. Now, if only Mouse didn't spring up and start barking!

"I've been practicing the lute for Her Majesty and studying the notes of a new song to play and sing," I said sweetly. "The volume you lent me is especially helpful, since it provides the notes for both parts—my lute as well as voice. I can't wait to perform it for Queen Mary."

The older woman hesitated. "Very well, then. I hope you have chosen something cheerful."

I bowed. "Aye. It's written by Her Majesty's great-uncle, King Henry. It's called 'Pastime with Good Company.'"

She stared, wondering if I mocked her. "Humph!"

And then she was gone in a swirl of silk.

The Plot to Kill a Queen

I let my breath out and sat next to Mouse. My hands shook as I stroked her soft ears.

"You are the best spy and the best little dog who ever lived, Mousie," I whispered. "You played your part of a sleepy spaniel perfectly. I worried you might yap at that scary lady, but you were magnificent!"

Mouse just opened her mouth and yawned.

Perhaps I was a coward. But I stayed in my room the rest of the day and transported myself to Aethelflaed's time. Somehow, fleeing Viking invaders seemed easier than venturing out into the menacing stone corridors around me.

Fifteen

Act II, Scene 15, Castle courtyard

"What's down there?" I asked Alice casually as Mouse and I walked with her to the henhouse one morning. I pointed at an open cellar doorway near one of the outside sculleries used for washing pots and utensils.

A week had passed since Elizabeth Curle had come to my room, another week in which I still had no answers. I was stuck, as stuck as we'd been in that coach that day in the ditch, except there was no one to help me out of the mire. I felt more anxious each day. What if the plot those men were discussing at the inn playhouse had been going forward all this time? What if the danger to Elizabeth was increasing with each passing day?

The Plot to Kill a Queen

Alice shrugged. "Oh, that's a storeroom for extra grain and root vegetables. Why do you ask?"

"Oh, it's just that since my play is set in medieval times, I've gotten curious about this old castle and how people lived three hundred years ago." That, I thought, wasn't a complete lie.

"Pooh!" said Alice. "This old fortress may be fine to look at, but as for living here . . . Every day I dread winter more."

"At least the food is good. That's certainly Mouse's favorite thing," I said. "Look at my little pooch. I believe she's getting plumper by the day—thanks to the meals you bring us."

Since everyone ate leftovers from Mary's elaborate meals, Mouse and I had sampled duck, venison, trout, salmon, and herring. I'd had my first fancy French tart with glazed pears. And Mousekin adored the Scottish shortbread cookies shaped into triangles called petticoat tails. I hoped Horace knew how to make them so he could bake Mouse a special treat back in London.

Eggs collected, we headed back toward the kitchen, past the usual early morning bustle in the courtyard. We passed Monsieur Nau speaking with the driver of a cart, a list in his hand.

He turned to beam at us. "Bonjour, mademoiselles. You're looking well today."

"Now there's a gentleman who doesn't think it beneath him to greet servants," said Alice, giggling a little.

"What is Claude Nau doing anyway?" I asked Alice. "I often see him in the courtyard." I'd come to realize Claude must be more than a messenger: Most mornings I saw him checking supplies coming into the castle.

"Oh, he helps Master Melville track what the French chefs order for their recipes. It's no easy matter to make sixty-four different dishes a day," Alice said. "And since Claude speaks French, the chefs tell him what they need—meats, vegetables, fish, and the like. He works with Master Melville on the orders, then examines the deliveries to be sure all is correct."

I considered this. It was possible letters could be hidden under a cartload of vegetables or a brace of pheasants, but I'd never seen Claude Nau—or anyone else—get close enough to slip anything into a cart or wagon. Claude merely strolled around, smiling, chatting, and checking his list.

As for Elizabeth Curle, though I rarely saw her in the courtyard, she often came to the servants' breakfast room to give orders to the Scottish staff. But since they spoke in Scots, I couldn't understand. Nor did I think she'd be discussing such secret matters there.

Time was running short. And I had no proof, except a

feeling in my gut that Elizabeth Curle had the determination, strength of mind, and deadly resolve needed to plot to kill Elizabeth and put her beloved Mary on the throne.

Act II, Scene 16, Queen's presence chamber

One afternoon in late October Mary had a new visitor: Bessie's grandmother.

The magnificently imposing Bess of Hardwick was also the Countess of Shrewsbury and one of Mary's jailers, along with her husband the earl. The noblewoman had come to admire Mary's needlework and apologize for being too busy of late to sew alongside her.

She gushed over a piece the queen had just finished, but frowned when Mary handed her a new sketch.

"What do you think?" Mary asked. "Have I captured the essence of the matter?"

Bess of Hardwick hesitated. "It is somber, Your Majesty. I confess I prefer the creatures whose images you copy from books—tigers from foreign lands and sea creatures like dolphins."

"This design sheds light on things close to my heart," Mary replied so quietly I barely heard her.

I wished I could have seen the sketch they were discussing, but Mary had placed it on the table, facedown. The moment passed. Their conversation turned to the colors of embroidery thread to be ordered next.

Shortly after Bessie's grandmother left, Claude Nau arrived, impeccably dressed as always. Mary smiled at him warmly and he made a gracious bow. As I'd seen him do before, he stopped to pay his compliments to Bessie and they exchanged a whispered conversation.

And once again, Mistress Curle stood before the dais and took a note from his hand. Perhaps, I thought, Claude comes here simply to deliver the daily menu.

After he left, Mary surveyed the room. She called out, "Mistress Bassano, you have met my sister queen, have you not? Come forward and tell me what you think. Is this sketch for my new embroidery a fair depiction of Elizabeth's heart?"

Near me, Bessie hissed, "Go on, then."

I made my way to Mary's worktable and bowed. Other embroidery panels displayed around the presence chamber depicted scenes from nature: birds, trees, honeybees, flowers, and fish. This image was different.

The sketch showed a cat with a crown on her head next to a mouse that clearly wanted to run away. It had no chance: Its tail was firmly pinned down by one of the cat's paws. Meanwhile, the cat had a menacing, satisfied expression on her face.

The Plot to Kill a Queen

"I shall use gold threads for the cat," Mary informed me. "Is my sister queen's hair still ginger?"

"Um... Yes, Your Majesty. Yes it is," I mumbled, still staring at the sketch.

No wonder Bessie's grandmother had called it somber. Queen Elizabeth was the cat; Mary the mouse. Mary craved liberty but knew the cat was there, relentless and powerful. The image was indeed somber—even dismal. It was like a glimpse into Queen Mary's heart.

"What do you think of my design, Mistress Bassano?"

I hesitated for a moment, unsure what to say. "Truly, Your Majesty, your skill in design is unsurpassed. Your art will impress for generations to come."

"A safe answer." She sighed. "Some days, only these threads of color brighten my days. It's sad to think that though I was born to rule a nation, my only legacy will be this art."

"But it is beautiful, extraordinary art, Your Majesty," I said. "And art transcends time."

"You have strange thoughts in your head for a young girl," said the queen. "Tell me, did your mother teach you to do needlework?"

"No, Your Majesty," I said. "My mother died when I was a baby, just weeks old. My father taught me the lute, but he's gone now."

"Ah, so you know loss too." She paused a moment. "My

son lives, yet I cannot see or even correspond with him, which causes me great heartache. Perhaps you can write a song for me about that, child. Will you do that?"

I swallowed hard. "I shall, Your Majesty. I promise."

- INTERMISSION -

Castle Lovers!

This seems a good time to tell you a little more about Sheffield Castle and Sheffield Manor, where Mary, Queen of Scots, spent most of her captivity.

The castle was constructed around 1270 and demolished in 1644. Cleaning a castle with primitive drainage was a huge undertaking. When that happened, Mary and her entourage were moved two miles to the smaller, more comfortable Sheffield Manor, also owned by the Earl of Shrewsbury.

Today, Sheffield Manor Lodge is a local history museum with guided tours of the remains of the manor gatehouse, where Mary stayed at times. You can watch a ten-minute video tour of Sheffield Manor and even get a peek at Tudor toilets here: www.youtube.com/watch?v=LbKKsFNx9gQ.

Now to Act III.

❧ Act III ❧
Vigilant as a Cat

Mary, Queen of Scots, gave the ginger cat a crown. Look closely. The mouse is trapped—its tail caught under one of the cat's paws.

"TUT, NEVER FEAR ME. I AM AS VIGILANT AS A CAT TO STEAL CREAM."
—William Shakespeare, Henry IV, Part I, Act IV, Scene 2

Sixteen

Act III, Scene 1, Turret room, All Hallows' Eve

October 31: All Hallows' Eve. Perhaps Mouse sensed something eerie about this day. Perhaps she had eaten too many petticoat tails at supper.

Or perhaps Mousekin was simply a better spy than me. Whatever the reason, my spaniel scratched at the door extremely early, even before the pounding of the guards' drums. I rubbed my eyes sleepily. Alice had given me extra candles and more oil for my lamp. I'd stayed up late and finished the play. Now it was tucked inside the writing box.

Tonight I planned to read the final pages to Alice. Talking to her about the story had helped me create the scenes: when Aethelflaed spots the Viking invaders, when

King Alfred's followers flee through the night, when the exhausted king falls asleep in a swineherd's hut, and when the princess appears to save the day.

At least I had done this: *The Princess Saves the Cakes* was now an actual play with a beginning, a middle, and an end.

As for my own tale here at Sheffield Castle, I felt bogged down in the middle with no resolution in sight: I still had not a single clue how Mary's coded letters were being smuggled. And I'd just about given up trying to find any. Whatever method Elizabeth Curle—or even someone else—was using, I simply wasn't able to discover it.

"Mouse, it's awful early," I complained as I dressed quickly and threw my cloak over my shoulders. "Did you eat something that made your tummy sick?"

Woof! she cried, insistent. *Woof!*

As I made my way sleepily down the cold, dark stairwells, I tried not to think what could happen if the plot I'd heard those men talking about weeks ago in London went forward. An attack on Queen Elizabeth might come from anyone or anywhere.

It will be my fault, I thought. *My failure may cause the death of a queen.*

The Plot to Kill a Queen

🪶 Act III, Scene 2, Castle courtyard, (very) early morning

We stepped out of the castle into the dark, foggy courtyard. Even with my woolen cloak, I shivered. I trailed Mousekin as she wandered here and there. Then, perhaps hearing an actual mouse, she made a beeline for the side of the yard, close to the castle, where some barrels, wheels, crates, and a broken cart had been piled up.

Mouse stopped and stared at a large horse that had just halted near a cellar door. The horse pulled a cart with one large wooden keg on it. It was an especially early delivery, true. But perhaps the brewer simply wanted to get started on his daily run so he could be home that night before dark. After all, it was All Hallows' Eve.

Mouse stood rooted. She growled at the big horse.

"Mousekin, come away," I called. For one of the few times in her life, she obeyed, and started to meander over to where I stood.

Still drowsy, my thoughts elsewhere, I almost turned away. But instead I watched Mouse, just to make sure she didn't decide to go back and tease the cart horse. That's when I noticed someone had emerged to join the brewer.

I stepped quickly behind some stacked barrels, out of sight. At first I thought the person was a servant who'd come to help carry the barrel. But no. This wasn't a kitchen helper. This man wore a soft velvet hat.

Who is it and why is he here? I wondered.

The mist was too thick to see much, so I sprinted a little closer, hiding behind another odd-shaped collection of broken crates and barrels. The two men leaned close, murmuring. I couldn't hear much, but my view was better.

And when the man from the castle turned his head, I could just barely make out a thin face and a stylish, distinctive mustache in the mist.

Claude Nau. Claude Nau? My world shifted. Could it be?

∞

I had to get closer—but not so close I'd be spotted. I rubbed my eyes, trying to find other objects I could hide behind. The early fog was always thick here because the castle sat just above the confluence of the River Sheaf and the River Don. This morning it was like trying to peer through a freezing gray veil. That was an advantage too: I was less likely to be seen.

Claude was standing close to the brewer. There was one more pile of debris near me, and I sprang toward it, crouching, the way I imagined a soldier on a battlefield seeking cover might do. I held my breath, afraid to make even the slightest sound.

The Plot to Kill a Queen

And then I saw Claude reach across and twist a round wooden knob at the bottom of the wooden keg close to the cart. The brewer might do that to adjust a leaky spigot, but why was the queen's personal secretary fiddling with the barrel?

I caught a white flash. Paper? Whatever it was, it was out of the barrel in a flash and into Claude's small leather purse that hung from his belt. With a swift motion, he drew something out from the same bag and slipped it into the barrel.

The secret communication method, a hidden compartment near the spigot of a brewer's barrel, revealed at last!

Someone had built a hidden compartment in the keg—a compartment large enough to hide a letter.

This is it! I thought triumphantly. *This* is how they're smuggling the letters. The exchange could be made in a matter of seconds. And in the busy loading area off the kitchens, with everyone rushing and bustling to unload barrels, boxes, and crates of vegetables, a few seconds is all it would take.

The man bringing the beer was either an avid supporter of Mary—or simply being paid well for his involvement and silence. The brewer clearly was in on it, though. A stocky, broad-shouldered man, he moved to shield Claude's movements from the rest of the courtyard.

I wondered how many days a week the cart made a delivery: probably at least once or twice. With water being unsafe to drink, the residents of Sheffield Castle went through gallons of beer each day. But I'd never seen it. This delivery came early, under the cover of darkness, even before Mary's guards beat their drums at five.

And if it wasn't for Mousekin, I'd never have discovered it at all.

The exchange completed, the two men stood together. To anyone observing, they were simply enjoying a friendly chat, which was normal for Claude Nau. No one would

The Plot to Kill a Queen

think anything of it. He always greeted tradesmen and inspected deliveries. It was part of his job.

Claude Nau also spoke French. I'd been so wrong! Of course, he was the logical person not only to communicate with Mary's French chefs—but also her supporters in France. And then I remembered something else: On the occasions when I'd been asked to play while Mary and her retainers ate their evening supper, Claude had been seated with other members of her senior staff.

Coordinating with the French chefs was part of his duties, to be sure. But what if he was also charged with coding and decoding Mary's secret letters?

I'd suspected Elizabeth Curle because she was fearsome and formidable. The charming Frenchman had fooled me—and probably many others.

And now I had proof: evidence I'd seen with my own eyes.

∞

The two men were still chatting. Claude spoke in a low voice to the driver. I strained to hear. Only two words were clear: "Five days."

Five days. Five days? What could that mean?

Claude might simply be asking the brewer to return

in five days for Mary's next letters. Yet what if it signified something else? What if an attempt on Elizabeth's life was set to take place in five days' time?

I sat back on my heels, my breath coming fast. If Elizabeth truly was in danger this soon, I couldn't wait for Mrs. Hughes to return in a few days to fetch me. Even if I sent a message in care of the innkeeper asking that she come earlier, I couldn't know when that would be.

Nor could I get a message to Sir Francis. I didn't want to try to pass a note to Alice to give to her friend Nathan; I couldn't take the chance she might be caught and lose her position. I didn't want to get Alice in trouble.

I could think of only one thing to do: I had to leave today. Now.

Seventeen

🖋 **Act III, Scene 2 continued, Castle courtyard, (very) early morning**

Now. I had to leave now. But how?

I stood in the predawn darkness, my mind racing. Thanks to Fannie's pin money, I had enough to take a coach to London. I couldn't make that journey as an unaccompanied female of course. But I still had my disguise. I'd have to ride in a coach by day as a lad and sleep in haylofts in the stables of coaching inns at night. It seemed the only way.

"Let's go. We must leave, Mousekin," I whispered. "Mouse?"

A moment ago, she'd been sniffing quietly underfoot, nosing about for dropped crumbs.

Yap! Yap! Yap! Oh no! Mouse had spotted one of the kitchen cats strolling across the courtyard. And if there was one thing Mousekin couldn't resist besides food, it was the chance to charge a cat.

"Mousekin, no!" I hissed. I didn't want to spring out from behind my hiding place. I couldn't be spotted and suspected of eavesdropping.

But now Mouse was streaking off, barking, heading straight for Claude Nau and the brewer—and the cat. *Yap! Yap! Yap!*

At that moment, Alice emerged from the castle and set out to cross the courtyard, her white cap fresh and clean, egg basket on one arm. She was on her way to the henhouse. But seeing Mouse, she made a detour and scurried after the little spaniel. With one smooth motion, Alice leaned over and scooped up Mouse, then walked back toward the castle.

"Oh, Mousie. You can't have that cat for breakfast," I heard her say from my hiding place. "Come inside and I'll give you something better. Did you sneak out while your mistress was still sleeping?"

I let out my breath. Alice had saved me from being discovered just by being Alice—a kind, good friend.

The Plot to Kill a Queen

Soon after, two servants emerged from the castle. Rather than unload the keg itself, the beer was drained into barrels. And that made sense too. The brewer would take his empty keg away. But, of course, it wouldn't be entirely empty. It still held a coded letter from Mary, Queen of Scots.

Claude Nau disappeared inside through a different door than the one by the servants' table, probably on his way to his chamber to hide the letter he'd just received. *Perhaps Claude Nau is Mary's Thomas Phillips*, I thought. *Though a much slyer and more charming decipherer.* A deceiver. I wondered, for a moment, if he was also deceiving Bessie about his admiration for her. I'd probably never know.

I waited a few more moments, then hurried into the kitchens. *I haven't been seen*, I thought with relief, my heart pounding. It had been a close call. A very close call.

Now I only had to leave in a way no one would remark on, and take my secret with me. In the kitchen, I reached out to take Mouse from Alice's arms. She raised her eyebrows in surprise at my sudden appearance.

I leaned close and whispered, "Thanks for keeping this little one safe, Alice. I wonder, could you get free for a few minutes? Please?"

Alice nodded, her clear eyes wide with questions. Outwardly she was her usual cheerful self as she handed over my furry friend. "I'll grab a small loaf and come up as soon as I can."

Act III, Scene 3, Turret room

I ran up the steps holding Mousekin under one arm, my mind racing.

What if the details of an attempt on Elizabeth's life were in the very letters exchanged this morning?

What if Mary had given her approval of actions to kill the queen, and that letter was now on its way to her chief supporters here, maybe even the men I'd seen at the playhouse in London?

I knew what I had to do.

The journey to London took three days. If I could catch a coach today from the Rose and Crown Inn, I could reach London in enough time to alert Sir Francis. Oh, if only I were a lad and could ride a horse!

"It's a good thing I packed my disguise," I murmured to Mouse, putting her down on the bed.

By the time Alice arrived, two pieces of paper sat on my table. I'd nearly finished changing into my disguise—the servant lad's clothes I'd kept hidden in my satchel for weeks now.

Alice stepped in and I rushed to close the door behind her.

"What . . . what are you wearing, Emilia?"

Alice was so startled by my appearance that she dropped the bread she held. Mouse pounced on it. That

The Plot to Kill a Queen

was fine with me. I was too nervous to eat. And Mouse certainly had earned her breakfast.

"I can't explain, Alice," I said, tucking my hair up under the boys' cap. I'd have to be more careful than that day at the playhouse, when Will Shakespeare had seen through my disguise. "I must leave this morning and get to Sheffield without anyone realizing I've gone."

"But . . . but why?" Alice frowned. "Are you all right, Emilia?"

"I'm well. It's nothing like that. It's . . ." I paused. "It's better if I don't tell you the details, but I promise you it's nothing bad. I'm simply aiding a friend who serves Queen Elizabeth. And you could help me, if you're willing."

"I always wondered if you were here as something more than a lute player. You're so different from anyone I've ever met." Alice searched my face, then seemed to make up her mind. She nodded. "I trust you, Emilia. How can I help?"

I gestured to the table. "There. That folded message on the right is addressed to Andrew Melville. It tells the master of the queen's household that I've departed. I wrote that I received a message from the innkeeper that I'm needed in London to attend a sick cousin. I thank him for the queen's hospitality and ask that my trunk be sent to the Rose and Crown Inn later."

"But those things aren't true, are they?" Alice said.

Then she nodded. "All right. What do you want me to do with the note?"

"Could you bring it to his office later this morning? He's busy with other matters; I doubt he'll give my departure a second thought.

"However, even if he does decide to check my story and finds that I didn't leave the castle this morning with the innkeeper, it won't matter. I'll be gone by then, well on my way."

"To London?"

I nodded, grabbing her hands. "Yes, that's why I must dress in disguise. I must leave today. Please, Alice. Perhaps you can say you brought coal to my chamber and found this folded note with his name on it. I wouldn't ask you to lie if it wasn't important."

"I know that." Alice squeezed my hands. Then she picked up the note and slipped it into her pocket. "I won't see you again, will I?"

I hugged her thin frame. "We don't know that. Maybe you'll come to London someday as the seamstress for a great noble family."

Alice smiled and pointed to my lute case. "What about your beautiful lute?"

My heart sank. "I don't think . . . I can't manage that and Mouse too. I hope Master Melville will send it to the inn later with my trunk."

The Plot to Kill a Queen

I wondered if that would happen. I thought of all the discarded objects in the attic of the Bell Savage Inn. Would Andrew Melville's ill temper cause him to simply toss my belongings in some abandoned room of the castle?

"I can't take my writing box or the pages of my play either, Alice. It will be hard enough to tuck Mouse under my cloak," I said sadly. "The paper would crinkle and make noise in case we have to hide. You keep it, and my writing box too. I put the box back in the hiding place after writing this note."

"I'm not very good at reading and writing, Emilia. My father taught me some letters but . . ."

"Then you can practice. That's how I got better playing the lute," I told her. "I'll write to you in care of the inn. We may not see each other again, but we can keep in touch. You're a true friend, Alice."

Alice gestured to the table. "What about that other paper?"

I snatched it up. "I need to deliver this message myself."

"You do look like a servant lad," Alice said, giving Mousekin and me a last hug. "Are you sure you'll be all right?"

I nodded. "Yes, no one will be looking for me. I'll be fine." *It will be easy*, I told myself, *because no one notices servants.*

Then I gave Alice one last hug and whispered, "I hope you enjoy reading my play!"

Eighteen

♟ Act III, Scene 4, Mary's presence chamber

"No one notices servants," Mrs. Hughes had told me. And that was true—except when servants were discovered trespassing where they shouldn't be.

I'd reached the hallway of Mary's presence chamber without being seen. By now I knew most of the back stairwells and corridors, so I managed to reach the hallway of Mary's presence chamber without being seen. As I was about to enter, I hesitated, glancing up and down the corridor. It was empty. No guards in sight. At least I'd timed that well. Some guards were probably still at breakfast. Others might be on duty in Mary's private garden.

I knew the queen often visited the birds in her aviary

in the mornings, just as she'd been doing the first day we'd met. She and her ladies wouldn't gather here in the presence chamber until the midday meal.

I peered in. The great hall was deserted. Should I go in or just slip away now?

I stared at the paper in my hand. Perhaps I should've asked Alice to bring it to the master of the household. But if I'd done that, I doubted this message would ever reach Mary. Besides, although she was likely scheming against Elizabeth, I had written this for the queen's eyes only.

I couldn't really say why. Maybe it was partly that Mary had been kind to Mouse and me. Partly that I felt sorry for her and could understand her sorrow. Mary had been forced from her son when he was a baby, just as I'd lost my own mother. She was alone, as I was alone now without Papa.

Most of all, though, it was that I'd made a promise.

"Keep your promises," Papa told me, just days before he died. "Grow up to be a woman of your word, Emilia."

Keeping that promise would turn out to be dangerous.

∞

As we entered, Mouse whined a little and struggled to get free, aware of Geddon's scent. "Quiet now," I whispered. "Geddon isn't here. I'm afraid you can't play with your friend today."

Or ever again.

I tiptoed across the brilliantly colored carpet; the excellent boots Horace had found for me made no sound. I went straight to Mary's worktable. She might write letters secreted in her bed chamber. But these embroidery panels were the heart of her creativity, something that would last, perhaps even for seven hundred years.

I spotted several pencil sketches for the vigilant cat and the mouse panel strewn across on the table. The embroidery panel itself was here too.

Mary had been working diligently on her needlework. The cat and mouse were already outlined in thread. And she'd starting on the cat's watchful, piercing eyes—eyes that looked very feminine indeed. I could see the outline of the little mouse too, its tail firmly imprisoned by the cat's paw.

I lifted one corner and tucked my song under the panel's canvas backing so that a scrap of the paper peeked out. She would notice it at once. I knew no one else, not even Elizabeth Curle, would dare touch Mary's needlework. With luck she would discover my gift later, after the midday dinner.

By then, Mistress Curle would have been informed that I'd left. Whether that lady conspired with Claude Nau or not, I couldn't know. But I now realized Claude's appearances in the presence chamber were a kind of theatrical

The Plot to Kill a Queen

performance too. Before the other ladies and any visitors who might be there, he deferred to Elizabeth Curle.

Yet probably, late at night, it was Claude Nau who scribbled by candlelight to turn Mary's desperate bids to her supporters for freedom into secret code.

And even with that, I had risked coming into this chamber once more. For this song was my parting gift. A gift and perhaps an apology too, though I hoped Mary would never learn I'd been a spy under her roof. I'd written the song she'd requested and set the lyrics to the tune Papa had taught me.

> "The Queen's Lament" (to the tune of "Greensleeves")
> Alas, my son, you do me wrong
> To cast me off discourteously
> For I have loved you oh so long
> And yearn still for your company
> This, this is my queen's lament
> My heart is full of sorrow
> I once flew free but now I sit
> a poor and broken sparrow.
> My little child was my delight
> I did not wish to leave him.

Deborah Hopkinson

> *But far from Scotland now I'm kept*
> *With no hope of returning.*
> *This, this is my queen's lament*
> *My heart is full of sorrow*
> *My flame, once bright, is dimming now*
> *my fire turned to ashes.*

As I turned away, my hand brushed one of the pencil sketches and it fluttered to the floor. I picked it up and gazed at it for a second, heart pounding, seized by an emotion I couldn't put into words.

This seemed an early, discarded sketch. It was rough, unfinished, with only the outlines of the cat and mouse visible. But in the quiet of that great, sad room, I felt as though the picture was about me. I was that mouse.

The large, powerful cat was everything about the world that kept me pinned down. It wasn't just me, I knew. It was all women and girls. It was families who had little and toiled for others. And anyone who looked different from the wealthy nobles who ruled over everyone else.

I had to have it.

I didn't think Mary would miss this sketch. She'd done several others, before creating one final pencil design that now lay right next to her embroidery.

And so I snatched it up, folded it, and stuffed it under Mouse. Then I sprinted across the bright carpets and out of the chamber.

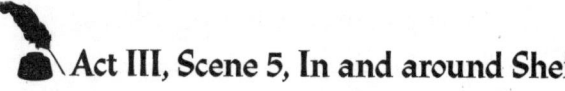 Act III, Scene 5, In and around Sheffield Castle

I almost got away. But it seems my tail was caught here too.

Just as I emerged from the presence chamber, a guard came swaggering down the hallway from the other direction. Instantly I knew him. This was the guard with the broken nose who had glared at me so intensely.

Would he recognize me now? Or would he assume I was simply a servant lad bringing coal or candles or doing some small cleaning task?

"You there, lad! What were you doing in there?" he hollered.

Without stopping, I turned my head slightly and mumbled, "Mistress Curle wanted more candles, sir."

I kept walking. I didn't break into a run until I turned a corner of the hallway. Just before I did, I overheard the first guard say to a second man who'd come up behind him, "A lad just came out of the chamber there. He acted suspicious. I think he may have stolen something."

"Is he one of the servants?"

"I'm not sure. I'm not sure who it is."

Deborah Hopkinson

– ASIDE: A BIT ABOUT EAVESDROPPING –

> **Eavesdropping** is a dramatic device in which a character overhears the conversation of others.

I know, this isn't the best moment to stop the action. But I wanted to mention that eavesdropping (as I just did with the conversation of the two guards) is a dramatic device often used by playwrights.

As an eavesdropper, I presumed the guards' conversation was accurate and that I was unseen, just as I had eavesdropped on the two men at the Bell Salvage Inn and on Claude Nau and the brewer in the courtyard.

But eavesdropping characters who think they're getting accurate information can be mistaken. The people they're listening to might realize they're being overheard and so they deliberately mislead the eavesdropper.

You won't be surprised to learn that our friend Will Shakespeare liked to make use of eavesdropping in his plays, especially in *Much Ado about Nothing*.

That, though, is a comedy. And at the moment I was beginning to think the plot of my tale was rapidly taking a turn for the worse.

It was turning into a tragedy.

Nineteen

🪶 **Act III, Scene 5 continued, In and around Sheffield Castle**

I didn't wait to hear more.

"Not a peep or a squeak, Mousie," I panted, keeping her snug against me with one hand as I scrambled down a smelly old stairwell. There were no handholds, and I braced my other hand against the wall to keep my balance.

I found a back way out and slipped out of the castle near the kitchens, but through a different door than the one by the servants' breakfast table. It seemed like a lifetime ago I'd seen Claude Nau and the brewer in the courtyard, yet it was early still.

For a second, I hesitated. Should I hide in a cart and leave the castle grounds that way? Immediately I rejected the notion. The wagons might be searched. Even if someone like Alice's friend Nathan was willing to conceal me in his cart, I didn't want to get Alice or Nathan or an innocent farmer into trouble.

And so I made my escape on foot, hugging the castle wall, walking purposefully through the entrance gate. Luckily, the moat bridge was empty. No horses and carts were approaching. And so far, I didn't think I was being followed.

Would they actually come after me? I couldn't be sure. The two guards might just shrug off chasing someone who looked like a servant, even if they didn't recognize him.

But that guard with the broken nose worried me. If he had been turned to work for Mary's cause, he might have recognized me as the lute girl from London. He might be suspicious enough to pursue me, to question me and discover what I knew.

A few more steps and I was on the bridge over the moat—the only way in and out of the castle.

"Once we cross this bridge, Mouse, I think we'll be safe," I whispered. I tried not to breathe in the rank smell of the moat. "It will mean no one is pursuing us. We can race through the deer park and be on our way to London in a few hours. You'll get to see lots of sheep again."

All at once I heard shouts and the *clomp, clomp, clomp* of heavy boots.

The Plot to Kill a Queen

Act III, Scene 6, Moat bridge, Sheffield Castle

So here we are, where we began. Do you remember? (And I do think this scene fits better here, in our third and final act.)

Yes, this is how I got here, racing across the bridge, guards after me, running out of options, about to turn myself in. What would happen then? I'd be caught wearing a disguise, with a stolen sketch made by Mary, Queen of Scots.

The guards might well lash out without asking questions. Though I thought (or at least I hoped) it was more likely I'd be captured and turned over to the Earl of Shrewsbury or a local magistrate. If that happened, Sir Francis would eventually hear of my plight and come to my rescue.

But days would pass. More than five days—and in those five days the plot to kill the queen might succeed.

And then, just as I was about to turn and give myself up, I saw a chance. A slim one, but a chance.

"Hold on, Mousekin," I whispered, tightening the wrap that kept the little dog safe against my chest.

It was a lone scraggly bush, clinging to the earthen embankment on my right. The bush was growing a little below the lip of the cliff. If I could lower myself down it, I could hang onto its branches, traverse the bank, and hide under the bridge—anything to keep from falling into the moat.

I sprinted off the end of the bridge onto muddy grass. At the cliff edge, I used my hand to smooth over my footprints. Then I launched myself over.

At least I knew to go down backward. When I was little, Papa had once lifted me up into a tree in the palace gardens so I could pluck a pretty apple. "Papa, let me climb down myself," I'd begged.

"Not that way, Emilia," he'd said with a laugh, taking the apple from my hand and guiding my arms and legs into position. "Turn around. Never look down or you'll topple headfirst."

Never look down. I lowered myself, inch by inch, grabbing hold of the bush and stabbing the toes of my boots into the dirt. Suddenly my foot slipped and I dangled in empty space for a horrible second.

Maybe this wasn't such a good idea. I could almost hear Horace saying, "I do wish you'd stop to think first before plunging ahead, Emilia."

I couldn't give up now. Aethelflaed, warrior queen of Mercia, wouldn't have. Nor would Elizabeth. And, I now knew, neither would Mary, Queen of Scots. I'd learned that much in my time here.

At last! My toe found purchase—a narrow bit of stone. I

dug in and kept moving. I wasn't out of danger yet. Anyone glancing over the edge of the bridge could see me. I had to get underneath it. I took one step to the side, then another, holding on to branches to keep from slipping. I closed my nose against the smell.

Suddenly, like an unexpected gift, I spied a shallow, hollowed-out space directly below the bridge. Another few feet and I'd pressed myself into it. I let go a shaky breath. I was safe—for now anyway.

I wondered if some long-ago thief had scraped out this hiding place. I silently thanked him—or her. I was a thief now too. I'd stolen a precious secret, a secret I had to protect. A secret I hoped no one knew I'd found.

After all, that's what spies do.

"Are you sure you want to go?" Fannie had asked me weeks ago. "You don't have to take on this mission, Emilia."

"I want to," I told her. "I gave your father my word. And once I make up my mind to do something, I keep trying, even if the world doesn't approve, and no one else believes I can do it. I have to believe in myself."

Now I lifted Mouse's long soft ear. "Let's be brave, determined warriors, Mouse."

Mousekin was never the smartest spaniel in the realm, but on this day she must have sensed our predicament. Not a whimper escaped her.

Deborah Hopkinson

My body was still tensed like a lute string about to snap. I heard boots shuffling to a stop over my head. I recognized the voice of the guard with the broken nose. "He must be heading toward town. Follow me and spread out."

I don't know whose heart was beating harder as we huddled under that bridge, listening to the scrapes and thumps of the boots overhead. I put my nose next to Mouse's soft wet one. Her little tongue reached out to lick my face.

I listened until the footsteps faded. I had escaped immediate capture but my problem remained the same: I was stuck under a bridge in enemy territory.

"Now what do we do, my dear Mousekin?" I whispered. I couldn't stay here long. I wanted to leave today for London.

I waited a minute. Two. Five. All was quiet. I was about to move when I heard more footsteps, not so heavy this time. Someone was trotting across the bridge. The boots came to a halt right over my head. Then they went to the side. It sounded as if someone had lowered themselves, perhaps trying to peer under the bridge.

I shrunk closer into the crevice. *No one can see me from up there*, I told myself. *Just stay still and don't move.*

I heard a voice, an astonishing voice. A voice I knew.

Twenty

Act III, Scene 6 continued, Moat bridge, Sheffield Castle

"I know you like to plunge into things," said the whispered voice. "But dangling over a stinky moat seems to be going a bit far."

For a few seconds I couldn't believe my ears. Was I dreaming? Mousekin, on the other hand, was not confused. She began to wriggle. She let loose a tiny muffled bark and wagged her tail furiously.

"Em, there's not much time," said the voice. "Come out while it's clear. I'll help you up the side of the cliff."

"Horace?" My head spun. Horace was here! Mousekin whined in excitement. I emerged from the narrow crevice and looked up. There he was: a lad with his cap pulled down over his eyes.

"But . . . but how? How are you here?"

"Questions later," Horace said. "Right now we need to move fast before the guards come back or some delivery wagon arrives. Can you traverse the side of the embankment to hold on to that bush? Then I'll pull you up."

Horace lay on his stomach on the grass and reached his hand down. Holding on to my reliable bush (I owed that bush my life!), I maneuvered close enough to grab his hand. A moment later, Mouse and I were sprawled on the grass.

"Now what?" I asked. "Do you have a plan?"

"As it happens, I do. We've got to sprint across the fields to a side road. We'll meet someone there."

"Is it far?"

"Not too far for a little dog to run." Horace lifted Mouse out of the sling and she gave him ecstatic sloppy kisses. "Now, Mousekin, there will be some gingerbread for you if you run like the wind and don't chase any rabbits along the way. And no barking."

And so we ran.

The Plot to Kill a Queen

🖋 Act III, Scene 7, Great Deer Park near Sheffield Castle

The grass and spent wildflowers and underbrush were cold and wet from the heavy mist. We were still near the rivers, which made for the thick, lingering fog. But in the distance, toward Sheffield town, I could see the mist starting to lift.

At first, I kept turning around, expecting to see guards chasing us. Sometimes we stopped to catch our breath, listening hard. Once, we startled a doe and two half-grown fawns. Otherwise, it was a gray cold fall morning, the last day of October.

At least for now, the searchers were expecting me to head straight through the deer park to Sheffield. Horace was leading us to the left, cutting cross-country at a right angle to the main road.

Twenty minutes later, we stomped through some brush next to a narrow dirt road. Horace drew me down behind a large oak. "There's a turnout just here. That's where we'll meet. You won't be out of danger even then, so you'll have to hide. You and Mouse both."

I nodded, my heart still pounding. I put a hand on his arm and whispered, "By the way, before I forget. Thank you again for these boots, Horace. I would've fallen into the moat without them."

He wrinkled his nose. "That wouldn't have been very pleasant."

"But how?" I cried. "Have you been here the entire time? And how did you get away from your job?"

"Sir Francis arranged it. I left the same morning as you on horseback, and arrived in Sheffield a day before you did," Horace whispered. "You're not very observant for a spy, Em. You didn't recognize me when Nathan and I pulled your coach out of the ditch. And I've been making regular trips to the castle with Nathan in his wagon."

"So that was you, with your cap always pulled down low covering your face," I exclaimed.

My head spun. First Fannie. Now Horace. What next?

"Wait. Have you . . . have you been one of Sir Francis's intelligence gatherers all along?" I demanded. "Are you the one who told him I'd gone to the Bell Savage Inn?" I remembered how Sir Francis had known that detail—a detail I hadn't mentioned to Fannie.

"Aye, I pick up a lot of gossip in the palace kitchens. There are deliverymen as well as the servants of foreign visitors who come in requesting special meals," Horace said, leaning back against the tree and scratching Mouse's ears.

"Sir Francis came to Whitehall to meet with the queen after you played for her that day. He's known to be especially fond of my gingerbread, and sometimes sends for me, supposedly to get a special treat and give me a small tip."

"But really that's when you report to him," I said.

"It is. By the time I met with Sir Francis that day, Fannie had already told him you'd overheard those two men. He asked me if I knew anything more, since he's aware we are friends. I actually didn't know about the men because I didn't see you after you got back.

"But I *did* have to tell him it was thanks to me that you'd gotten a disguise to go to the Bell Savage Inn. Sorry about that, Em. So Sir Francis asked me to come here . . . just in case you needed help," Horace said.

"Did you think I couldn't do it alone, Horace?" I cried.

"No, it's not that," he said. "There are other reasons for me to be here too. I'll tell you more later. As for the plot, though, I haven't discovered anything. But I'm guessing you have, because here you are, escaping in disguise."

That explanation would also have to wait for later. A faint rumble caught my ear. "I hear a wagon," I whispered.

Horace poked his head up carefully. "That's him."

The clip-clop of the horse's hooves drew closer. I heard a low "Whoa."

Silence. Horace gave a low whistle, which was answered right away. "I'll go first," he murmured. "Just to be sure. When I whistle, you come."

I found myself holding Mousekin close. I suppose I should've been more frightened: I had no idea what might happen next. But nothing seemed as bad as almost falling off that hill into the moat.

At Horace's whistle, I joined him beside a farm wagon on the side of the road. The driver doffed his cap. "You're Nathan, Alice's friend."

"Nice to meet you formally, Mistress Bassano," said Nathan, with a little bow. He gave Horace a little punch in the ribs. "I've heard a lot about you from this fellow, as well as from Alice and my mum."

His mother?

Before I could ask, Nathan had climbed up to the wagon bed and held out a hand to me. "Let's not tarry. This is a back road, little used. But for all we know, the guards may fan out to check all carts and wagons heading into Sheffield."

"What if they do stop wagons to search for me?"

Horace and Nathan exchanged grins. "They won't find you, Em," said Horace.

Nathan peeled back some cloth coverings, then fiddled with the wagon bed to expose a hidden compartment in the bottom of the wagon. "It's not a long drive. When we reach the Rose and Crown, we'll bring the wagon into the back area of the stable."

"What then?" I asked. "I need to go back to London—today."

Nathan nodded. "Mum will handle that. You should be able to make the mail coach. It leaves the inn around noon. You'll be in London in three days."

I scrambled up into the wagon and began to lower myself into the hidden compartment.

"Sorry about the delay, by the way," Nathan said. "Alice said you had to have that, so we had to find a minute when the coast was clear to load it. She put it in a sack."

I climbed in and put my hand out to touch the sack. Through the cloth I knew exactly what it was.

Tears spilled down my cheeks. Alice had smuggled Papa's lute out of the castle.

Twenty-One

Act III, Scene 8, In a wagon, then the Rose and Crown courtyard

"I told you I wouldn't let you fall in the moat," I whispered to Mouse as we bounced along. I kept one hand on my lute case. I didn't like being in this closed space, but touching something Papa had made and loved made it easier.

If only I'd been able to bring my script with me. But I couldn't have taken the chance of pages rattling as those guards stood above my head on the bridge. There wouldn't be time to rewrite my play, but I had proved to myself I could do it. And in some strange way, I felt that the warrior spirit of that long-ago princess was with me.

Before long, the outside noises grew louder. I heard

people's voices, the clomping of hooves, the creak of other carts and wagons.

Mouse wriggled against me. She was ready to escape this hiding place too.

※

Finally, the wagon halted in what I guessed was the coaching inn's courtyard. I waited, expecting that any moment the wagon would move into the stables and we could get out.

Then I realized there were guards here, interrogating the innkeeper. "Haven't seen any suspicious boys," he told them.

At least they weren't looking for me, Emilia. Alice wouldn't have delivered my false message to Andrew Melville yet. That meant I still had a few hours before I was missed.

Finally, when I thought I couldn't stand being confined another moment, the wagon moved slowly. Outside sounds were muffled. I thought we must be inside the stables now. In a moment more, the boards were pried open. I sat up and found three pairs of eyes staring at me.

Horace, of course. And Nathan.

It took me a few moments to place the third person. She seemed familiar, yet also different. She wore a light blue gown and a few curls escaped from her cap. She was smiling brightly.

Nathan grinned and held out his hand to help me up. "Emilia, I think you've already met my mother, though perhaps under a different name."

"Hello, Emilia," said the woman. "Congratulations. I'm guessing you left early because your mission was a success."

I gulped. "Mrs. Hughes?"

She smiled. "Field is my married name."

Twenty-Two

 Act III, Scene 9, Sir Francis Walsingham's study

A few days later I found myself knocking on the door of Sir Francis's study.

"Emilia, we're delighted to have you back," he said, gesturing me to the sturdy wooden chair before his desk. I curtsied, sat, and smoothed my gown. I'd brought Mouse with me. After all, she'd been essential to our mission.

"I understand your departure was a bit hasty and that your trunk was left behind," he said. "It's already been moved to the Rose and Crown Inn and will be arriving here by coach."

"Thank you, sir. It *was* hasty," I said. "I'd barely arrived at the inn when I boarded the coach for London. A cousin of Mrs. Hughes . . . Mrs. Field, rather . . . was already coming, and I traveled as her maid in the last seat on the coach."

There had been no time for questions—or answers. Mrs. Field—the bright, vibrant wife of Daniel Field, innkeeper, had found me clothes, and I'd used the name Emily again. I'd scarcely had time to change, let alone talk to Horace.

Sir Francis leaned forward and steepled his fingers. "Now, tell me what you found."

I took a breath. "I believe Claude Nau is in charge of coding and decoding her letters. He seems to have Mary's confidence. The letters are smuggled in and out of the castle inside a secret compartment in a beer cask. I'm fairly sure the brewer himself makes the deliveries rather than a servant.

"I caught only part of what Claude Nau and the brewer said. But when I heard them say five days, I felt I should leave right away," I told him. "Just in case . . . in case an attack might take place soon. In two days now.

"I tried to cover my departure so that no one on Mary's staff realized I'd discovered anything."

"Well done." Sir Francis nodded. "You were right to act quickly. And, I am sure you're correct about Claude Nau too. I believe he is from Paris and has many connections in France.

"As for this imminent threat, Queen Elizabeth loves to

ride, so we will insist she stay inside for the next few days and increase her guards until we can discover more."

"What will happen to the brewer now?" I asked. "Will he be arrested? And will Claude Nau be sent back to France?"

"The brewer?" Sir Francis gave the briefest shake of his head. "Oh, no. We'll leave both the brewer and Claude Nau in place and let them go on smuggling Mary's coded correspondence just as before."

"But... but don't you want to stop them from plotting?" I cried. "You won't even arrest the brewer?"

"Why should I arrest the man, when I can pay him to continue—and see each letter before it reaches Mary's conspirators?" Sir Francis gazed at me with an amused gleam in his sad, hooded eyes. "Remember, Emilia, anyone can be bought. Daniel Field is already in touch with the man."

"I'm not sure I understand," I said.

"Thomas Phillips can decode anything Claude Nau can conjure up. This way, we will know what the plotters are planning; we may be able to influence the course of events to achieve our ends.

"So you see, Emilia," said the spymaster, "the plot to kill a queen is now about to get underway in earnest."

Before I left Sir Francis, I wanted to ask him about Papa. How had my chaperone known him? And why had Sir Francis offered to take me in?

"Your father and his brothers had strong ties to Italy. And since there have been plots ever since Mary arrived in England, your family has been quite helpful," Sir Francis told me. "In fact, as I recall, when you were still a baby, your father undertook a trip to Europe in the service of Elizabeth."

"If I was so little, who took care of me while he was gone?" I wondered.

Sir Francis frowned. "Let me think. Ah, I know. You were born in January of 1569, were you not? The Fields were still living in London then. We helped them buy the inn in Sheffield later, in 1570, after Queen Mary was moved to Sheffield Castle.

"Yes, I remember now," Sir Francis continued. "Their son Nathan was about two. And Horace is about the same age as you. So you stayed with them."

I croaked. "Horace?"

"Yes, Horace Field. A brave family, the Fields, don't you agree?"

The Plot to Kill a Queen

Act III, Scene 10, Our bedchamber

"What do you think your father meant?" I asked Fannie later.

Fannie had been sharing palace gossip, though I noticed most of her stories involved Philip Sidney. "About what?" she asked.

"That the plot to kill a queen is about to begin."

"Oh, Emilia, don't you see?"

I shook my head. "See what?"

"My father believes the only way to keep Elizabeth safe is if Mary no longer poses a threat. That's why he'll let Queen Mary continue with her letters—and be sure he intercepts them. He will watch and pounce at the right moment, waiting until she makes a fatal mistake and goes too far. It may be a matter of weeks, or months, or even years.

"Though, I suppose, he may not even wait for her to make a mistake all on her own," she added.

I took a breath, her meaning suddenly clear. Sir Francis was also plotting to kill a queen.

"I just wish it could be . . . different. I wish there was a way to keep both queens safe. Perhaps if they could meet, they would find a way, as two women, two sister queens.

"But that won't happen." I said with a sigh. "I suppose I'm always imagining a different world."

Fannie hugged me. "Knowing you, Emilia, I think

you'll always imagine a world where women wear breeches, travel alone through the streets, and perform onstage."

"I believe I'd like that world very much," I told her.

Act III, Scene 11, The same chamber, evening of November 16

Fannie had gone to dance at the palace, but I'd stayed home. My cousin Arthur had invited me to join his musicians the next day for a special performance in honor of Queene's Day. I hadn't taken out my lute since I'd returned from Sheffield Castle and needed to practice.

Mousekin sprawled on the bed, her muzzle resting comfortably on her paws. She seemed content to be home. "Are you ready to listen to me practice 'Greensleeves' and 'Pastime with Good Company,' Mouse?"

There was something else I wanted to do as well. I'd stashed my disguise in the bottom of my satchel, and slipped Mary's sketch in there too.

Now I opened my lute case. I'd decided to tuck the sketch into the pocket Papa had made on the inside of the case to hold pages of written music. I wasn't sure what I would do with it, but it was a reminder, I supposed, that each and every person had a wish to be free.

But when I reached in, I frowned. The pocket was

The Plot to Kill a Queen

stuffed full. I had brought extra music to Sheffield. After I'd learned those pieces, I'd put the sheets of paper in my trunk and had brought the partbook with me to the presence chamber.

So what could this be?

I drew out the packet and laughed aloud.

Twenty-Three

Act III, Scene 12, London, various roads and an office

Only the servants were awake when I slipped out of the house on Seething Lane the next morning. I considered leaving Mouse behind. But she'd begun this journey with me, and she should see it through.

I didn't rush. We'd have to wait for the office to open, so I had time. And though I didn't plan to go there, my steps took me to the Tower of London. I picked up Mousekin so she wouldn't run off and get under the hooves of a passing horse, and stood gazing at the imposing fortress.

"Somewhere over there on Tower Green is where Anne Boleyn, mother of Elizabeth, had her head taken off. And perhaps Mary's life will end that way too. I suspect she'll want Geddon with her, if it comes to that," I said softly.

I lifted Mouse's silky ear. "But as I told Fannie, I would wish for a different ending for Mary, just as I'd like other things to be different. Why not? Yet I can only try to bend my world a little in the direction I hope it will go."

∞

When the building opened, I tucked Mousekin under my short walking cape and marched inside. Today I was playing the part of the messenger boy.

I found the Office of the Master of the Revels and approached a clerk seated at a desk. "Pardon me, sir, my master wishes to enter his play into consideration for the royal competition."

The man removed his spectacles and pushed a ledger toward me. "Sign your master's name here and the title of his play."

"Um . . . can my master remain anonymous?"

"I'm afraid not."

I dared not write E. Bassano on it, for the Bassano name was known at court, and I might be found out and (once again) prove to be an embarrassment. No, I would have to put some other name on it. Then I remembered.

"Very well." I took the quill he offered, dipped it in the inkpot, and wrote with a flourish, thoroughly enjoying myself. (Girls did not get many chances to sign official records, after all.)

"Very good," said the clerk. "Now his name will be recorded in the historical record."

But will this record survive for ten, twenty, or five hundred years? I doubted it. More than likely, the person whose name I wrote would never know it had been done, nor would anyone ever go looking for it.

Though, of course, I couldn't be absolutely sure. Perhaps someone in a future time will be curious about how we live, the words we write, the clothes we wear, about the fates of queens. Maybe even about my fate.

"You will take good care not to lose the play?" I asked. It had, after all, made the journey to London hidden in a lute case—thanks to Alice.

I had stayed up late the night before to make a copy. I planned to make another one too and make sure Horace got it to his brother, Nathan, to give to Alice. Maybe they would read it together.

"Aye, we'll keep it safe," he replied. "The name of the winner will be posted outside this office in five days' time. Will your master wish to be notified by letter as well?"

"No, that won't be necessary," I said. "He has left

London and won't even be able to see it performed should it win."

"Ah, that's unfortunate," he said. "I'm sure it's sweet to see one's own words brought to life. But writers have the satisfaction of their pens, do they not? And perhaps that is enough."

"Yes, indeed," I agreed. "After all, the play's the thing."

※

Mousekin and I left the office and went outside. London was still waking up. It was a rare crisp day. The city stretched ahead of us. We would take our time walking home. Tonight I would perform again on the Minstrels' Balcony. I would be a little sad, thinking about the fate of one queen, but glad that my own queen was safe.

Perhaps that was part of what I'd gleaned from my mission—that the world was a complicated, hard place. But it was still my world. And I intended to go through it in my own way, asking questions and finding my own path.

※

As for seeing *The Princess Saves the Cakes* being performed at court, I'm afraid my play did not win. Though I suppose it's still possible some scholar might find the ledger I signed and feel they've made a spectacular discovery—the first play by Master William Shakespeare from Stratford, who'd offered up his name to me one day as a kind of jest.

"If you wish, you may use my name on your play, Emilia Bassano. It will be our secret," Will Shakespeare had whispered at the Bell Savage Inn that day as he took his leave. "If I achieve my dream, we might confound scholars who will wonder how I could have submitted my play in November of 1582, the same month I was being married to Anne Hathaway in Stratford."

- ASIDE -

Dear reader, if you in the future are able to find footnotes to history, you will discover that on December the twenty-sixth of 1582, a comedy entitled *A Game of Cards* was performed at court by a troupe of boy actors, the Children of the Chapel Royal.

I did see it. I think my play was better!

Act III, Scene 13, Walsingham home, December 27

As for *The Princess Saves the Cakes*, Will Shakespeare had it right. It seems that all along I'd been writing a play for the enjoyment of family and friends.

Two days after Christmas, Sir Francis and Lady Walsingham opened their home to my (rather large) extended Bassano family. Children of friends and servants attended as well. I was surprised that Sir Francis agreed. But it only took a little persuasion. In the end, he quipped, "Why not?"

As for the players, it was a true ensemble production and delighted the audience young and old.

> An ensemble is a group of musicians, actors, or dancers who perform together.

Fannie made a wonderful Princess Aethelflaed, of course. Sir Francis himself took on the role of King Alfred, opposite Lady Walsingham's Queen Ealhswith.

Horace, back from an extended visit with his family in Sheffield, made a very silly peasant woman, baking his oatcakes and making all the littlest Bassanos chortle with laughter (and yes, his mum is the one who taught him to make gingerbread, so naturally we had that as our treat after the performance).

Fannie's Philip Sidney was a magnificent King Guthrum. To my astonishment, Thomas Phillips agreed to be young Prince Edward and was rather droll. My adult Bassano cousins delighted their children as Vikings and thanes.

I provided musical interludes, with faithful Mousekin beside me raising her voice in a yowl. (Though it must be said that at the time she couldn't resist scrambling out onto the performance area to assist the various actors.)

I also served as playwright, director, and producer for the opening (and closing) night performance of *The Princess Saves the Cakes*.

I found that I enjoyed being in charge. I liked it very much indeed.

A director serves as the primary visionary and unifying force behind a theatrical production.

Finale

> A **finale** is the last section of a piece of music or performance.

AS FOR MY OWN PART I CARE NOT FOR DEATH, FOR ALL MEN ARE MORTAL; AND THOUGH I BE A WOMAN YET I HAVE AS GOOD A COURAGE ANSWERABLE TO MY PLACE AS EVER MY FATHER HAD.

—Elizabeth I, 1566

A few days into the new year, Fannie handed me a folded letter. "Father received this from Her Majesty. It's for you."

I held it gingerly. "Go on, Em. Open it," Fannie urged.

I shook my head and handed it back. "You read it, Fannie." I grabbed Mouse. "Mousekin and I will listen."

To the court musician Emilia Bassano,

Sir Francis informs me that you have done a great service to the realm, just as your father before you proved loyal and devoted. I look forward to hearing you sing and play in this new year of 1583. Your rendition of "Greensleeves" pleases me greatly. I hope I may rely on your courage and ingenuity in the future, should the need arise.

Curtain Call

> A **curtain call** is the appearance of one or more performers onstage after a performance to acknowledge the audience's applause.

And so, dear reader, I leave you now. I shall imagine you closing your book and returning to life in a world full of wonders I can't begin to imagine.

One final word, however. Do you remember our prologue, where I included a phrase coined by Will Shakespeare? It was: "What's past is prologue."*

Deborah Hopkinson

The words are from his play *The Tempest*, in which Antonio tells Sebastian, "What's past is prologue."

I take his meaning to be that all that has happened before leads to this moment, when Antonio and Sebastian plot to kill King Alonso and make Sebastian king instead. (It doesn't work out.)

The full quotation is this: "Whereof what's past is prologue; what to come, in yours and my discharge."

I, for one, don't believe Will is saying that the past must predict our future; we are not bound to repeat past mistakes or ways of doing things.

Rather, the past simply brings us to the now, to this moment. And then it's up to us to go forward—to make good choices—to make the present and future our own as best we can.

That is what I've tried to do—always challenging the script someone else would have liked to write for me.

Do the same, dear reader. Follow your own script: Live each day in your own way, as only you can. Why not?

---

*A NOTE FROM THE PRODUCERS. A version of Will Shakespeare's original phrase "What's past is prologue" is inscribed on a statue of a young woman, entitled Future, by Robert Aitken. The statue graces the entrance of the National Archives Building in Washington, DC. A woman holds an open book, symbolizing what is yet to be written. On the other side of the entrance is an old man with a closed book. You can guess the title of this statue: Past.

I think Emilia would have liked these statues, don't you?

Production Notes

Two Queens and a Deadly Rivalry

The Plot to Kill a Queen is historical fiction. Although the story was inspired by real people and events, it is entirely made up, and I have not attempted to replicate Elizabethan language or Scottish or French accents. I've also taken liberties with the facts of Emilia Bassano's life: She never encountered Shakespeare; spied for Sir Francis Walsingham; met Mary, Queen of Scots; or wrote a play. I simply decided to give her these adventures. Why not?

However, there is some actual history behind our story. It takes place in the fall and winter of 1582, when Queen Elizabeth I had been on the throne twenty-four years. Mary, Queen of Scots, was Elizabeth's cousin. Since she had a legitimate claim to the English throne, she was a threat even in captivity. You can find more facts in the timeline in this section.

Mary had a complicated and tumultuous life. Mary, a devoted Catholic, was forced off her throne by Protestant factions in 1567. Her infant son, James, was named king. Mary fled to England in 1568, hoping Elizabeth would aid her in regaining her throne. Instead, Mary was held captive for years, often at Sheffield Castle, before being beheaded in 1587 following the Babington Plot, a plan to assassinate Queen Elizabeth I. (A sad footnote to history is that Mary hid her dog Geddon under her robes on the day of her execution. It's said he later died, heartbroken.)

The method of smuggling letters in a beer keg was used in 1586 in the Babington Plot. Sir Francis Walsingham employed many spies and double agents and was able to intercept Mary's correspondence without the queen or her conspirators knowing their letters were being read. In the end, Walsingham and his assistant Thomas Phelippes (sometimes also spelled Phillips as it is in our story) deciphered an intercepted coded letter smuggled in a beer keg. Phillips added a forged postscript in the same code, supposedly from Mary, asking conspirator Anthony Babington for the names of those prepared to help her escape and kill Elizabeth. Thinking the request came from Mary, he provided the details. That letter was evidence enough to entrap Mary and the conspirators, leading to the execution of Mary and six plotters.

To read more about the Babington Plot, visit www.thehistorypress.co.uk/articles/a-beginner-s-guide-to-the-babington-plot.

Although Elizabeth was reluctant to kill a fellow queen, Mary was beheaded on February 8, 1587. Some historians speculate that if Elizabeth and Mary had met in person, they might have reached an agreement that would have given Mary her freedom and avoided her death. We'll never know. We do know Sir Francis Walsingham didn't believe Elizabeth was safe so long as Mary was alive. Thus, our title: *The Plot to Kill a Queen*. Were both queens a target?

Since Sheffield Castle is long gone, I've imagined what Emilia's stay there was like, though I've included a few details historians have uncovered, such as the guards beating drums in the early morning, the number of dishes served for the elaborate meals, and the fact that Mary did, indeed, bathe in white wine.

It's also true that Mary was an accomplished needlewoman. You can see some of her embroideries online at the Victoria and Albert Museum: www.vam.ac.uk/articles/prison-embroideries-mary-queen-of-scots. To see a film about the cat-and-mouse embroidery that appears in our story, visit www.rct.uk/resources/video-embroidery-by-mary-queen-of-scots.

Elizabethan Theater

Elizabethan England was a time of intrigue and espionage, and it was also an era when literature and theater thrived. And while I've invented the royal play competition, masques and plays were often performed at Elizabeth's

Shakespeare's Globe, a reconstruction of the 1599 Globe Theatre on the south banks of the River Thames in London, attracts thousands of theater lovers each year.

court, especially during the holidays. Masques were a form of entertainment that became popular during the time of King Henry VIII. In a masque, players in disguise combined verse, music, and dance to tell a story, often from mythology. Unlike plays, women were able to perform in masques.

As for William Shakespeare, there are two periods of his life historians refer to as the "lost years." The first is between 1578 and November 1582, when he married Anne Hathaway at the age of eighteen. In our story, I've imagined Will visiting London during this first lost period just prior to his marriage. You can find out more about Shakespeare's life and Tudor customs at the Shakespeare Birthplace Trust: www.shakespeare.org.uk.

Only white men performed onstage in Elizabethan times. In 1661, the law in England was changed to allow female professional actors. In 1828, Ira Aldridge became the first Black actor to portray the title character in Shakespeare's *Othello*. Today, of course, Shakespeare's plays are performed by diverse casts the world over. There have been all-female productions, all-Black and all-Black female casts, as well as productions by Native American and Indigenous theater companies. I think Emilia would approve!

The Real Emilia

I first learned of Emilia Bassano Lanyer (1569–1645)—sometimes spelled Aemilia Lanier—in 2019, after reading an article speculating about her possible links to Shakespeare, either as the author of his plays or the "Dark Lady" of Shakespeare's sonnets. While there is no evidence that Emilia knew Shakespeare or wrote his plays, there is still debate about whether Emilia and the Bassanos were Jews who converted publicly to avoid persecution but practiced their religion secretly.

Scholars who study Emilia Lanyer's life and work have

found that her father, Baptiste Bassano (sometimes John Baptiste), was part of a musical family of brothers from Italy who became court musicians in the Tudor court. Unlike in our story, Emilia's mother, an Englishwoman named Margaret Johnson, did not die when Emilia was a baby, nor did Emilia live with the Walsinghams, although she might have lived in the household of a noblewoman after her father's death when she was seven.

Emilia was one of the first English women to publish her own original work. Her book of poetry in 1611 had her full name on the title page and was dedicated to prominent women, making it the first book written by a woman and also dedicated to women. At a time when society accepted the notion that women were inferior, Emilia rejected that idea. Some scholars call her one of the first feminist writers in the West. Emilia also opened a school and ran it for two years after the death of her husband.

As for other female playwrights, in 1613, Elizabeth Cary became the first female in England to publish a play. Women in England had to wait much longer to enter the legal profession. It wasn't until 1922 that the first woman lawyer in England began practicing. And although some universities in England date back to the early thirteenth century, women weren't allowed to earn degrees there until the nineteenth century.

The real Emilia was probably nothing like the character

I've imagined in these pages. Yet, at some point, Emilia Bassano got the idea to assert herself as an author—to write a book and dedicate it to women, something no other woman in England had done. And perhaps, like our Emilia, she asked herself, Why not?

Petticoat Tails and Tudor Gingerbread (It's Not What You Think!)

Scotland is famous for its shortbread, and it's said that the French chefs of Mary, Queen of Scots, perfected and popularized this sweet treat in the sixteenth century. Today these cookies, also called petticoat tails, are a special holiday favorite. Shortbread cookies are often sold in tins. Or you can make your own!

Gingerbread in Tudor times was unlike the gingerbread we know today. It consisted of brown bread crumbs mixed with honey and spices, including ginger, nutmeg, and black pepper. It might be fun to try, but I know my dog Little Rue, who appears as Mouse in these pages, would prefer the modern version.

Selected Helpful Books

While this book wasn't intended to be historically accurate, the following resources were useful in writing about Elizabethan England.

Arnold, Catharine. *Globe: Life in Shakespeare's London*. New York: Simon & Schuster, 2015.

Budiansky, Stephen. *Her Majesty's Spymaster: Elizabeth I, Sir Francis Walsingham, and the Birth of Modern Espionage*. New York: Plume, 2005.

Cooper, John. *The Queen's Agent: Sir Francis Walsingham and the Rise of Espionage in Elizabethan England*. New York: Pegasus, 2012.

Grossman, Marshall, editor. *Aemilia Lanyer: Gender, Genre, and the Canon*. Lexington, KY: University Press of Kentucky, 1998.

Guy, John. *Mary, Queen of Scots: The True Life of Mary Stuart*. New York: Mariner Books, 2018.

Jones, Margaret C. *Founder, Fighter, Saxon Queen: Aethelflaed, Lady of the Mercians*. Barnsley, UK: Pen & Sword History, 2018.

Mortimer, Ian. *The Time Traveler's Guide to Elizabethan England*. New York: Penguin, 2012.

Porter, Stephen. *Shakespeare's London: Everyday Life in London 1580–1616*. Gloucestershire, UK: Amberley Publishing, 2011.

Templeman, David. *Mary, Queen of Scots: The Captive Queen in England, 1568–87*. Exeter, UK: Short Run Press, n.d.

Timeline of Actual Events

1533   Elizabeth I, the last Tudor monarch, is born.

1542   Mary Stuart, known as Mary, Queen of Scots, is born and becomes queen at six days old when her father, James V, dies.

1558   On November 17, Elizabeth ascends the throne.

1564   Playwright William Shakespeare is born in Stratford-upon-Avon.

1567   Frances Walsingham Burke is born. (Fannie in our story.) The same year, Queen Mary is forced to abdicate her throne and flees to England in 1568.

1568   Bessie Pierrepont is born and enters Queen Mary's service at age four. She may have had a relationship with Claude Nau.

1569   Emilia Bassano is born in January to Italian court musician Baptiste Bassano and Englishwoman Margaret Johnson.

1573   Sir Francis Walsingham becomes secretary of state.

1576   Emilia's father, Baptiste Bassano, dies when Emilia is seven.

1582 Eighteen-year-old William Shakespeare marries Anne Hathaway.
1583 Frances Walsingham marries Sir Philip Sidney, who later dies. She marries twice more.
1586 Anthony Babington is executed for his part in the Babington Plot. Secretary Claude Nau is among those arrested but later returns to France and is cleared of charges.
1587 Mary, Queen of Scots, is beheaded because of the Babington Plot.
1592 Emilia marries recorder player Alfonso Lanyer. Emilia had been the mistress of Lord Hunsdon, who probably arranged the marriage. She gave birth to a son, Henry, in 1593.
1599 The Globe Theatre is built on the south bank of the River Thames.
1603 Queen Elizabeth dies on March 24. Mary's son, James, becomes king of England, Ireland, and Scotland.
1611 Emilia publishes a book of poetry dedicated to prominent women.
1616 Shakespeare dies on April 23 (also thought to be his birthday) at age fifty-two.
1645 Emilia dies at age seventy-six.

The Princess Saves the Cakes

A ONE-ACT PLAY TO PERFORM WITH A COMPANY OF FRIENDS

—— from ——

The Plot to Kill a Queen
by Deborah Hopkinson

To my daughter, Rebekah, still the definitive Thomasina. —DH

You can put on this play in school, in your community, or in a private setting for family and friends. You don't need permission; we just ask that you please limit your use of the play to these types of performances and that you do not create and sell any other productions or products using any part of the play or in any way based on the play.

© 2023 Deborah Hopkinson. All rights reserved.

The Princess Saves the Cakes

Historical Note

The Princess Saves the Cakes, included in *The Plot to Kill a Queen*, was inspired by a tale dating back to AD 878, when England was a collection of regions rather than one unified country. That year, on January 6, as King Alfred and his followers celebrated Twelfth Night at his hunting lodge in Chippenham, Danish Vikings under King Guthrum launched a surprise attack.

Alfred, his family, and his followers (called thanes or theyns, which rhymes with *lanes*) fled to the village of Athelney in a swampy marshland area called the Somerset Levels. The king knew the marshes would hide them well and make it hard for the Vikings to mount an attack.

It was there, according to a story popularly called "King Alfred and the Cakes," that an exhausted King Alfred was mistaken for a common soldier and scolded by a swineherd's wife for falling asleep instead of turning her cakes (which may have been oatcakes or small loaves of bread) on the fire as she'd asked. At this time, of course, cooking was done over a fire. (Fans of the television series *Vikings* will

© 2023 Deborah Hopkinson. All rights reserved.

recognize a version of this event in season one.) The story is so famous there's even a small, lumpy black fungus nicknamed "King Alfred's cakes." The Anglo-Saxons avoided capture and in May of that year, King Alfred defeated King Guthrum in battle. That resulted in a treaty and a period of stability.

To read more about the legend, visit Dr. Paul Kelly's King Alfred blog: king-alfred.com/wp/2019/02/01/cakes/.

Children in England learn the story of King Alfred and the cakes.

In Emilia's play, Princess Aethelflaed, then about eight, takes a leading role. The real Aethelflaed grew up and married Aethelred, Lord of the Mercians. She ruled that region

© 2023 Deborah Hopkinson. All rights reserved.

of England after her husband's death in 911, fighting off more Viking attacks and becoming known as Lady of the Mercians. A female leader in medieval times was rare, making Aethelflaed's accomplishments even more remarkable.

Aethelflaed, Lady of the Mercians, lived from 870 to 918.

Performing This Play—Sets and Props

The Princess Saves the Cakes has a flexible number of speaking parts and actors; parts can be doubled or dialogue trimmed as needed. No stage sets are required—it can be performed on a stage, in a multipurpose room, even outside. Sets and props can be left to the imagination, although you may wish to make your own props from safe materials.

© 2023 Deborah Hopkinson. All rights reserved.

The English Heritage website has information about British history as well as arts and crafts activities such as building a cardboard castle. Check it out: www.english-heritage.org.uk. You can see reconstructed Anglo-Saxon helmets here: thethegns.blogspot.com/2020/05/the-five-anglo-saxon-helmets.html.

MAKE A CARDBOARD SHIELD
    www.english-heritage.org.uk/easter/preparing-for-easter-adventure-quests/how-to-make-a-cardboard-shield/

MAKE A SAFE SPEAR FROM PAPER
    www.instructables.com/Paper-Spear/

MAKE A MEDIEVAL HELMET
    www.english-heritage.org.uk/members-area/kids/kids-castles/medieval-helmet

Songs and Music

Music is a great addition to any performance. Here are some suggestions!

One song we know today might date all the way back to Aethelflaed's time. It's the ballad "Scarborough Fair," a variant of an old Scottish ballad, "The Elfin Knight."

There are also tunes that would have been popular in the Elizabethan period when Emilia lived. "Pastime with Good Company" was composed by Henry VIII, Queen Elizabeth I's father. In the story, Emilia often performed "Greensleeves,"

© 2023 Deborah Hopkinson. All rights reserved.

which was probably written around 1574. Links are provided should you wish to stream music in your production. Note: Websites do change and you may need to do an updated search.

For information and music for "Pastime with Good Company" and "Greensleeves," visit the London Symphony Orchestra: lso.co.uk/whats-on/alwaysplaying/read/1674-music-inspired-by-henry-viii-his-wives.html.

For Daniel Estrem's Renaissance lute instrumental version of "Greensleeves," visit YouTube: www.youtube.com/watch?v=OCpF2cwm_04.

For violinist Nigel Kennedy's rendition of "Scarborough Fair" with the English Chamber Orchestra, visit www.youtube.com/watch?v=UVFBVAtSZ7k.

For Roland Keunings's lute rendition of "Scarborough Fair," visit YouTube: www.youtube.com/watch?v=FIEXgbg5zCg.

For Viking songs, visit BBC School Radio: www.bbc.co.uk/teach/school-radio/music-ks2-viking-saga-songs-clips/zd4k92p.

© 2023 Deborah Hopkinson. All rights reserved.

The Princess Saves the Cakes

Cast, in Order of Appearance

The play has a flexible number of performers and speaking roles. There are 26 speaking parts, with some roles shared so no player has too much to memorize. This, of course, is optional and you may choose to combine speaking roles. Gender assignment is also optional. After all, there have been all-female productions of Shakespeare.

Narrator 1, 2, 3, 4, 5

West Saxons:

    Alfred 1, 2, King of the West Saxons

    West Saxon Thanes (or *followers*, sometimes spelled *thegns*; pronounced THANES, rhymes with *lanes*) 1, 2, 3, 4 (others as chorus)

    Princess Aethelflaed 1, 2, 3, King Alfred's daughter

    Ealhswith 1, 2, Wife of Alfred

    Edward, King Alfred's son

Vikings:

    Guthrum 1, 2, King of the Danish Vikings

© 2023 Deborah Hopkinson. All rights reserved.

Viking Warriors 1, 2, 3, 4 (add warrior roles as needed for chorus)

Villagers of Athelney in the Somerset Swamps:
Swineherder Parent A
Swineherder Parent B
Swineherders' Child

PRONUNCIATION GUIDE
Aethelflaed [Eth-el-fled]
Athelney village [Ath-el-knee]
Ealhswith [Eels-with]
Guthrum [Goo-thrum]

TIME: JANUARY 6, 878

SCENE 1
King Alfred's hunting lodge in Wessex

(*King Alfred and the Wessex cast are assembled onstage holding hands and dancing in a circle; the instrumental version of "Scarborough Fair" could be played at this time. Narrator 1 steps onstage in front of the revelers. The Wessex cast continues to circle behind Narrator 1.*)

Narrator 1: Happy Twelfth Night!

It's January sixth, the last night of holiday festivities. King Alfred and his followers are making merry at his

© 2023 Deborah Hopkinson. All rights reserved.

hunting lodge. They've feasted on bread, vegetables, and wild boar. YUM! Now they're dancing and singing.

But, alas, the year 878 will not have a happy start for the Saxons of Wessex.

Aethelflaed 1: (*Comes out of the circle and goes to the side of the stage as if stepping outside. Dancers move toward the back of the stage area.*) I'm so warm from dancing. The cold night air feels good. How dark it is without a moon!

But what's that light? It looks like a flickering torch. Who can it be? All our friends are here. Maybe a traveler is lost. I'll listen for cries of help. (*Tiptoes a few more steps and cups one ear to listen.*)

I don't hear voices. But I *do* hear the sound of boots crunching on the snow. I must tell my father, King Alfred! (*Aethelflaed darts inside and pulls on her father's arm.*)

King Alfred 1: What's wrong, Aethelflaed? Are you ill from dancing?

Aethelflaed 1: Father, come outside quickly! (*She leads him to the edge of the stage.*)

King Alfred 1: What is it, Daughter?

© 2023 Deborah Hopkinson. All rights reserved.

Aethelflaed 1: It's dark now, but I saw a torch flicker for a minute. Listen!

King Alfred 1: (*Listening.*) Marchers! This can mean only one thing.

King Alfred 1 and Aethelflaed 1 together: Viking invaders!

King Alfred 1: It's Guthrum, king of the Danish Vikings. He and his warriors mean to take us by surprise while we're having fun.
   We're outnumbered and not prepared for battle. Tell me, Daughter, what would you do?

Aethelflaed 1: (*Thinking.*) We should flee now and hide all winter. Then you can gather your followers and prepare to fight next spring.

King Alfred 1: A wise choice. According to our customs, your little brother Edward will inherit my throne someday. But you have the makings of a leader too.

Aethelflaed 1: Of course I do. And someday, I vow to defy those old customs and prove it. But for now, let's warn the others.

© 2023 Deborah Hopkinson. All rights reserved.

(*They step inside. King Alfred claps his hands to get attention. People stop dancing and gather in a half circle.*)

King Alfred 1: Gather round, friends and followers.

West Saxon Thane 1: What is it, King Alfred? We don't want to go to bed yet, do we, fellow Saxons?

West Saxon Followers: (*All together.*) No! We're having too much fun. Let's keep making merry!

King Alfred 1: (*Raising his hand for quiet.*) Quiet, friends. Our keen-eyed princess has spotted marchers in the distance. The king of Denmark and his Vikings are launching a surprise attack.

West Saxon Thane 2: But we're not ready! My spear isn't sharpened. It's duller than ditchwater.

West Saxon Thane 3: (*Scratching head.*) I'm not ready either. I can't decide what wood to use for my new shield.
    (*Turns to West Saxon Thane 4.*) What do you think, my friend? Should it be ash or alder? Or would maple or oak be better?

© 2023 Deborah Hopkinson. All rights reserved.

West Saxon Thane 4: Never mind that, my iron helmet is only half done. I don't want to end up with half a head!

(*West Saxons talk and argue among themselves excitedly.*)

King Alfred 1: Silence, please, my good thanes. We all agree: This is not the time for battle. Instead, we must escape. We'll walk through the night to the village of Athelney. It's in some marshy wetlands.

West Saxon Thane 1: Will the people of the marshlands hide us and give us food and shelter?

West Saxon Thane 2: I hope so. If I don't eat, I get grumpy as a bear.

West Saxon Thane 3: Me too. We'd better get there by breakfast.

King Alfred 1: Don't worry. The people there are generous and kind. Are you ready, Queen Ealhswith?

Queen Ealhswith 1: Yes, let's make haste. Put on your warm cloaks, everyone. Alfred, my husband, take this simple cape—not your royal one. If we're surrounded by Vikings, it will disguise you.

© 2023 Deborah Hopkinson. All rights reserved.

King Alfred 1: You are wise, Ealhswith. I think Aethelflaed gets her good sense from you.

Queen Ealhswith 1: Oh, I'm sure of it.
Now, everyone, grab bread and apples from the table for our children. We cannot yield to the Vikings. We must be strong!

West Saxon Thane 4: (*Grabbing.*) I'll take that last boar drumstick for the road.

West Saxons: (*All together, grabbing food from a pretend table, pretending to put on capes.*) Tonight we escape and hide. But we'll live to fight the Vikings another day!
(*West Saxons exit, stage right. When a performer is in the center facing the audience, that is called center stage. Stage right is to the performer's right; stage left to their left.*)

SCENE 2
King Guthrum and Vikings at the hunting lodge

Narrator 2: (*Steps onto empty stage.*)
Here comes King Guthrum of Denmark and his Viking warriors. Guthrum and other Viking leaders want to conquer all the regions of Saxon England. Most of all, the

© 2023 Deborah Hopkinson. All rights reserved.

Danish king wants to defeat Alfred, who rules the area called Wessex.

He won't be pleased to find Alfred and his friends have fled. Not only that, there's not much left to eat.

King Guthrum 1: (*Storming across the stage from stage left, wielding a spear—prop, or pretend—chanting as he enters.*)
Hear my fighting chant:
    My spear is sharp. Strong is my shield.
    King Alfred of Wessex: Yield, yield, yield!
(*Viking warriors enter stage left behind King Guthrum 1, also chanting.*)

Viking Warriors All:
My spear is sharp. Strong is my shield.
King Alfred of Wessex: Yield, yield, yield!
Yield, yield, yield! (*Stomp feet on last three yields.*)

King Guthrum 1: (*Holds up his spear calling for silence.*)
Silence, brave warriors! We're too late. The lodge is deserted. King Alfred and his followers have fled. They must have seen us coming.

(*Turns to Viking Warrior 1.*) I told you not to light that torch.

© 2023 Deborah Hopkinson. All rights reserved.

Viking Warrior 1: Sorry, my lord, it was just for a few minutes. I had a rock in my boot.

Viking Warrior 2: (*Pointing to the table.*) But look! They were here not long ago. This is the remains of their feast.

Viking Warrior 3: (*Going over to look at the table.*) Aye, but they ate all the good stuff. All that's left are turnips, cabbage, and parsnips. The wild boar is all gone!

Viking Warrior 4: UGH—turnips, cabbage, and parsnips! I knew I should've speared that fat squirrel and eaten it raw.

King Guthrum 1: Now, warriors, haven't I told you it's important to eat your vegetables? Finish this feast quickly. Then we'll track King Alfred and his followers through the night, the way a fox chases a rabbit.

They say he loves books more than battle. We'll see about that.

Vikings: (*All together, drinking and eating.*) Let's gobble up these turnips! Then we'll have the energy to chase down that book-loving king.

© 2023 Deborah Hopkinson. All rights reserved.

SCENE 3
In the woods and fields

(*Narrator steps to the front of the stage. Behind the narrator, King Alfred and the Wessex cast trudge across the stage, entering stage left. Queen Ealhswith, Edward, and Aethelflaed are at the rear.*)

Narrator 3: The people of Wessex escaped just in time. Now they must flee to the marshlands on this cold, moonless night. Young and old, they stumble through the snowy fields and the thick, dark woods.

But do they dare light their torches? No, they do not. They must not! They can't risk being spotted by the Vikings.

It's a long, hard walk, especially for young children like Prince Edward.

(*Narrator exits. Other Wessex cast exit stage right, leaving the queen, the prince, and the princess. Prince Edward trips and falls.*)

Prince Edward: The snow is so slippery. I can't keep up, Sister.

(*Aethelflaed 2 holds out a hand to help him up.*)

Aethelflaed 2: Here, take my hand, little brother. You can do it. (*They get up and walk toward Queen Ealhswith.*)

Prince Edward: How far is it, Mother?

© 2023 Deborah Hopkinson. All rights reserved.

Queen Ealhswith 2: We must walk all night, my brave children.

Prince Edward: But we've *already* been walking for hours, Mother! I'm tired and hungry. Is there anything to eat?

Queen Ealhswith 2: (*Takes pretend bread out of a pretend bag.*) Have some bread, Edward. Then you'll feel stronger.

Princess Aethelflaed 2: (*Looking ahead.*) Mother, may I run to catch up with the others and find Father?

Queen Ealhswith 2: You may, Daughter. But be careful. Watch out for wild boars and wolves.
    (*Aethelflaed runs off stage right.*)

Prince Edward: (*Looking around frantically.*) Mother, did you say wild boars and wolves? I'm ready to run too. Let's go!
    (*They exit stage right. King Guthrum and the Vikings enter from stage left.*)

King Guthrum 2: Viking warriors, keep up! This is no time for lagging. We haven't caught up to the Saxons yet.
    Remember our fighting chant? All together now!

© 2023 Deborah Hopkinson. All rights reserved.

King Guthrum 2 and Vikings:
>My spear is sharp. Strong is my shield.
>King Alfred of Wessex: Yield, yield, yield!
>Yield, yield, yield! (*Stomp feet on last three yields.*)

Viking Warrior 1: I wonder where King Alfred is headed.

Viking Warrior 2: I bet King Alfred wants to hide in the marshlands where it will be hard for us to find them.

Viking Warrior 3: You have to admit, that's a pretty smart strategy.

Viking Warrior 4: Hmm, I wonder if King Alfred read about it in a book.

King Guthrum 2: Silence, Vikings! I think it's about time for our marching chant. Do you remember how it goes?

Viking Warriors All: Less talking and more walking. Let's go! Stomp! Stomp! (*Stomp feet with the words* stomp, stomp.) (*They march off stage right.*)

© 2023 Deborah Hopkinson. All rights reserved.

SCENE 4
Village of Athelney, in the swamplands
[OPTIONAL SONG]

(*King Alfred 2 enters from stage left and moves slowly to center stage, where he eventually stumbles to one knee. West Saxons gather in a semi-circle at stage left and sing lyrics to the tune of "Scarborough Fair."*)

> What king is this
> so brave and bold
> who won't give up
> despite the cold.
> He leads his friends through this long night
> and gives them hope for peace and light.

Narrator 4: (*Steps onto empty stage.*) What a long, cold night! King Alfred has been leading his thanes hour after hour. He is worn down with worry. He has urged his friends on and given his last apples away to others.

Now Alfred is scouting ahead for the best place to hide. At dawn, he reaches the hilltop village of Athelney. Most people here keep sheep and swine and live in simple huts with thatched roofs. At last, Alfred spies a hut.

(*Narrator 4 exits. Swineherd family enters and comes center stage. Parent A gets busy mixing ingredients at a table. Parent B helps child on with shoes and cloak.*)

© 2023 Deborah Hopkinson. All rights reserved.

Swineherd Parent A: You must dress warm, my child. It looks to be another day of wet, cold snow.

Swineherd Child: Do we *have* to go out to the pen to feed the pigs? It's way too yucky outside.

Swineherd Parent B: Our pigs need us, and we need our pigs. We cannot let them go hungry just because we don't like the weather, now, can we?

Swineherd Child: I guess not. All right, piggies, here I come!

Swineherd Parent A: That's the spirit. And I'll have some nice hot oatcakes ready when you get back.

Swineherd Child: Yum! I love nice hot oatcakes.

(*Parent B and child exit stage right. Parent A shapes the small cakes. King Alfred enters stage left and stumbles with exhaustion outside the hut.*)

Swineherd Parent A: Who's there? Oh, a young warrior. You look tired and cold. Come in and sit by my fire to warm your bones. Here, have a cup of hot cider.

© 2023 Deborah Hopkinson. All rights reserved.

King Alfred 2: Thank you. I am a bit tired. I've been walking all night.

Swineherd Parent A: You're more than welcome to rest here, on the floor of our hut. But I wonder, since you're here . . .

King Alfred 2: (*Moving to sit down on the floor.*) Do you need my help with something?

Swineherd Parent A: Oh yes, if you wouldn't mind. I need to take my basket and go out to find firewood. Can you watch my oatcakes and take them off the fire before they burn?

King Alfred 2: I'd be happy to do that. Leave it to me.
(*Swineherd Parent A exits stage right, carrying a basket and picking up firewood along the way. King Alfred falls right asleep. Enter Aethelflaed 3 stage left.*)

Princess Aethelflaed 3: Where could Father be? Our friends stopped to rest. They said Father had gone ahead to find the village where we can hide.
(*Stops to look and notices hut.*) Oh, here's a small cottage. Should I knock? I hope they'll be friendly.

© 2023 Deborah Hopkinson. All rights reserved.

(*Comes closer and sniffs.*) It smells delicious. I think someone's baking oatcakes.

(*Knocks on door.*) Hmm, that's strange. No one is answering.

(*Sniffs again.*) But those cakes smell done. I wonder if someone forgot about them. I'll take a chance and go in. There's nothing worse than burnt oatcakes!

(*Princess Aethelflaed 3 walks into the hut.*)

Princess Aethelflaed 3: (*Looks around, then whispers.*) Oh, what's this? It's Father, fast asleep. Poor Father! He's all tired out with worry and walking.

It's not easy being a king. He needs his rest. And I bet he gave all his extra food to others.

But these oatcakes are definitely done! I'd better take them off the fire before they burn. Here's a mitten. And I can use this long-handled griddle to remove them from the heat. (*Pretends to take pan out of the fire and put it on the table.*)

Swineherd Parent A: (*Walks into the hut.*) Hello there. Who are you? And what are you doing?

Princess Aethelflaed 3: Oh, good morning! I'm just taking your cakes off the fire before they burn.

© 2023 Deborah Hopkinson. All rights reserved.

Swineherd Parent A: I asked that warrior to watch my cakes. Seems he didn't do a good job.

Princess Aethelflaed 3: (*Makes a little bow and puts her finger to her lips.*) Please don't wake the king. My father is so tired. I am sure he didn't mean to let you down.

Swineherd Parent A: The king? The king is in my hut? The man I asked to watch my cakes is Alfred, King of Wessex?

Princess Aethelflaed 3: Yes. We've been walking all night to escape the Vikings. My father brought us here to hide. He said the people of Athelney are good and kind. Now I see that is true with my own eyes.

Swineherd Parent A: Then you must be Princess Aethelflaed, the oldest child of Alfred and Ealhswith. Thank you for saving my cakes. Your parents must be proud of your good sense and quick wits. Would you like to eat one now?

Princess Aethelflaed 3: Oh, no thank you. My mother and little brother will be here soon. Edward is small and I'm sure he's very hungry by now. I'd rather you gave the cake to him.

© 2023 Deborah Hopkinson. All rights reserved.

Swineherd Parent A: Well, I'm impressed! You give food to your brother and you saved your father from a scolding by me. That wouldn't be the way he wants to be remembered.

King Alfred 2: (*Waking up and stretching.*) Oh, I'm sorry! I must have dozed off.

Swineherd Parent A: Luckily, your daughter saved you from a scolding.

King Alfred 2: Thank you, Princess. And I certainly wouldn't want the story of King Alfred burning the cakes to be the way I go down in history. (*King and princess hug.*)

EPILOGUE
(*All cast onstage in semicircle behind Guthrum, King Alfred, Ealhswith, Edward, and Aethelflaed. Guthrum and Alfred step out and bow to each other. Wessex and Viking warriors lay down shields, spears, and helmets, real or pretend.*)
   (*Narrator 5 enters from stage right or left.*)

Narrator 5: Spring has come. It's May 878. The great battle is over. King Alfred's plan worked. During the winter he gathered his warriors. The good people of Wessex came to King Alfred's aid and defeated the Vikings.

© 2023 Deborah Hopkinson. All rights reserved.

The kings signed a peace treaty called the Treaty of Alfred and Guthrum. Believe it or not, a copy still exists! Guthrum agreed to leave Wessex and mind his own business in East Anglia. From now on, King Alfred can devote himself to making laws, bringing books to Britain, and encouraging people to learn to read.

(*Princess Aethelflaed steps forward to front center stage.*)

Narrator 5: As for Aethelflaed, she grew up and married the Lord of the Mercians. When he died, she ruled in his stead, fighting off new Viking invasions.

The princess who saved the cakes became a warrior queen, Lady of the Mercians. Aethelflaed lived more than a thousand years ago. But we believe her message for us today would be clear.

All cast together: Be kind. Be generous. And most of all: SAVE THE CAKES!

(*All bow.*)

The End

© 2023 Deborah Hopkinson. All rights reserved.

Acknowledgments

My love of theater began in middle school, when our class performed a readers' theater rendition of *A Christmas Carol* by Charles Dickens. (I still remember the opening line: "Ebenezer Scrooge, hard and sharp as flint, solitary as an oyster!")

Though that's the extent of my own appearances onstage, one of my first professional jobs was as marketing director for the Manoa Valley Theatre in Honolulu, Hawaii, where I had the opportunity to meet volunteer actors and even a couple of nationally known playwrights.

Perhaps it's no surprise, then, that both my children grew up loving the theater. During high school, Dimitri enjoyed performing in summer musicals in the community amphitheater in Walla Walla, Washington, where we lived at the time.

Rebekah, now an educator, gave memorable performances in high school and community theater productions and still mounts plays with her students in Shelburne, Vermont. She served as the first reader to "The Princess Saves the Cakes" and I'm grateful for her valuable input.

Like a theater production, a book is a collaborative team effort. I'm grateful to my incomparable editor Lisa Sandell and my agent, Steven Malk, who believed that a book about Emilia Bassano wasn't a crazy idea. I'd also like to thank Courtney Donovan at Writers House and photo researcher Cian O'Day, who helped track down the illustrations in the book.

Thanks also to the entire Scholastic team who work so diligently to encourage reading. Thank you to Ellie Berger, David Levithan, Janell Harris, Rachel Feld, Katie Dutton, Aleah Gornbein, Seale Ballenger, Lizette Serrano, Emily Heddleson, Sabrina Montenigro, Maisha Johnson, Jana Haussman, Kelli Boyer, Laura Beets and the entire Book Fairs team, Amy Bradford, Mindy Stockfield, Emily Teresa, Cian O'Day, Cassy Price, Chris Stengel, Elizabeth Parisi, and many others. This book owes much to many talented professionals, including copyeditor Priscilla Eakeley. Thank you!

I wish to thank educators, teachers, librarians, and parents for encouraging young people to read, write—and perform.

To friends and family, your support means everything. I'm writing names in alphabetical order and hope

I don't forget anyone: Maya Abels and Stewart Holmes, Deniz Conger, Janice Fairbrother, Candace Fleming, Vicki Hemphill, Kristin Hill and Bill Carrick, C. Howard, Bonnie Johnson, Elisa Johnston, Fiona Kenshole, Katie Morrison, Sheridan Mosher, Rosanne Parry, Emily Picha, Kiara Sausedo, Judy Sierra, Becky and Greg Smith, Ellie Thomas, Pamela S. Turner, Teresa Vast and Michael Kieran, and Deborah Wiles and Jim Pearce.

To Andy, Dimitri, Rebekah, Eric, and Oliver—I love you more than words can say. Last but not least, I'll call for a round of applause for Little Rue, now making her second appearance in fiction. A cocker spaniel in real life, she, like Mousekin, is loyal and true. But as for visiting an old gloomy castle or hanging over a smelly moat, I think it's safe to say she prefers snoozing on her cozy dog bed next to me as I write.

Illustration Credits

Photos ©: iii, 1: Image Asset Management/www.agefotostock.com; vi–vii: PictureSheffield.com; ix: ivan-96/Getty Images; 9: Yale Center for British Art, Paul Mellon Collection; 10: Deborah Hopkinson; 17: Yale Center for British Art, Paul Mellon Fund; 19: Image 45862, used by permission of the Folger Shakespeare Library; 21: powerofforever/Getty Images; 45: Yale Center for British Art, In Memory of John V. McCarthy; 61: ilbusca/Getty Images; 75: duncan1890/Getty Images; 81: Yale Center for British Art, Paul Mellon Collection; 87: whitemay/Getty Images; 153: Jimlop collection/Alamy Stock Photo; 208: Nastasic/Getty Images; 209: The Picture Art Collection/Alamy Stock Photo; 221: duncan1890/Getty Images; 223: duncan1890/Getty Images; 224: Historia/Shutterstock. All other photos © Shutterstock.com.

About the Author

Deborah Hopkinson is the highly acclaimed author of thrilling, accessible, and compelling nonfiction for every reader. She has written over forty award-winning books, including *Titanic: Voices from the Disaster*, a finalist for the YALSA Excellence in Nonfiction Award and a Sibert Honor Book; *Race Against Death: The Greatest POW Rescue of World War II*; *D-Day: The World War II Invasion That Changed History*; *We Had to Be Brave: Escaping the Nazis on the Kindertransport*, which was a Kids' Book Choice Award Nominee and a Sydney Taylor Award Notable Book; *We Must Not Forget: Holocaust Stories of Survival and Resistance*, an NCTE Orbis Pictus Recommended title; and The Deadliest books, which are action-packed, photo-filled nonfiction titles about disasters throughout history and the impact of climate change in our time. Deborah lives outside Portland, Oregon, with her family, two dogs, a cat, and several canaries. Visit her online at www.deborahhopkinson.com.